I0621584

VETITUM

SOPHIA VENBOUE

Anickto Publishing

Anickto Publishing

(www.anickto.com)

Copyright © 2025 Sophia Venboue

All rights reserved.

The right of Sophia Venboue to be identified as the author of this work has been asserted by her in accordance with the Copyright, Designs and Patents Act 1988.

No part of this publication may be reproduced, stored in a retrieval system, or transmitted, in any form or by any means without prior written permission of the publisher, nor be otherwise circulated in any form of binding or cover other than that in which it is published and without a similar condition being imposed on the subsequent purchaser.

Paperback ISBN 978-1-9193582-0-8

eBook ISBN 978-1-9193582-1-5

Cover design by Sophia Venboue

CONTENTS

1

UNEXPECTED

Resting back on her pillow, Ellie wondered how it had come to this. How could something that had been so good, so beautiful, be evil or ugly? Had it really been that evil? She didn't have to close her eyes to see his face. She'd never forget it? The dimples in her cheeks deepened as she recalled that first day. A day when all would change. A day that would herald a tectonic shift in her perspective.

The day had begun a tense one, not helped by the restless night preceding it. Glistening dawn discovered her in the drawing room, watching as it gradually drove the dark of night from the scene. The cool air tickled her nostrils as she sought to calm herself. Could she make it a success? What would people think? More important, would Mummy approve? Why couldn't she be here? Why had she to go so early? Ellie winced, the stinging pain making her conscious of having bitten her lip. This was so unlike her. Normally confident in all she did, not accustomed to feeling undermined. But this was different. This was for Mummy. Her hand instinctively rested on her abdomen. She'd only known such turmoil once before. Then, she'd been younger and unable to think of a life without her loving mummy. Why, Why, had she gone? Where had she gone? The thoughts that had sat heavily that awful day. Daddy had done his best to explain, but she'd remained confused and bewildered. Shaking her head, Ellie dismissed the thoughts. This wasn't a time to allow such melancholy. She had to make this a success, for Mummy!

'You're up early darling.' The click of her spine was almost audible, the sudden intrusion into her thoughts having made her jump. 'Good morning, Daddy.' 'What's troubling you?', noting the tired tension in her normally fresh features, 'You're not worried about today? Are you? There's no need to be. You're great at organising things.' 'Thank you, Daddy, but this is different to anything I've done before. This is for Mummy. I don't want to let her down.' Wiping a tear from the corner of one eye. 'You'd never do that, darling. Come here.' Cradling her in the warmth of his arms. 'I miss her so much.' The tears no longer restrained. 'So do I darling, so do I.' The depressing burden on his heart revealing itself. 'Sorry Daddy. I didn't mean to stir all that up today.' 'It was inevitable. Today's the first time without her. We're both bound to feel it. But you're going to make her proud. I've been watching you prepare.

You're doing great. I know how pleased she'd be. Is.' 'Do you really think she can see us?' 'I like to think so.' Giving her a reassuring smile. 'Well, I'd better be getting on then. Otherwise, guests will arrive before we're ready. That'd never do.', wiping the tears from her cheeks. 'Okay. I'll just check all's well with the livestock. They don't understand anything about having a day off.' Finally managing to bring a smile to her face.

Glancing sidewards, Ellie was pleased to find her reflection didn't portray the restless night. The soothing warmth brushing her arms and the brilliant blue sky promised much. It was time. Time to accept her mother's mantel. Subconsciously lifting her right hand to her heart, Ellie again acknowledged the promise she'd made long ago. A promise made in the quiet of her heart. A promise to fulfil, to the best of her ability, all her mother's wishes and desires. Her silent prayer for help ascended. Calming her tumultuous stomach with a further deep intake of air, she stepped through the French doors. The pleasant, sweet yet sharp green leaf scent of freshly mowed grass swept up from the immaculately manicured lawn. An aroma she'd always enjoyed. Cheerful chirping along with angelic song enlivened the atmosphere. As did the bubble of conversations and loud encouragements coming from the front of the house. It all added to the promise of an excellent day.

Allowing the warmth of the rising sun to caress her delicate, uplifted features, Ellie permitted herself a few extra personal moments. The day would be hectic. This would probably be her only opportunity for time alone. Again, her silent prayer rose to the heavens, 'For you Mummy. For you.'. Intentionally prohibiting further tears, she straitened her back and lifted her shoulders. Time to take on her duties. Time to do the best she could. An oozing sensation in her stomach reminded her of how nervous she was. As if she need reminding.

The crunching of gravel beneath her feet announced her arrival into the melee. Standing centre stage, feet firmly planted, Arnold, the estate manager, fired out instructions in timely fashion. They'd spent the best part of the previous month going over and over the arrangements. Her mother had been master of such events and she'd wanted to ensure all would meet her expectations. Thankfully, Arnold had been involved before and could therefore provide some guidance. Heartfelt greetings and smiles were exchanged as each member of staff rushed to fulfil their part of the arrangements. They were, in truth, her extended family. Her parents had always made a point of everyone understanding that. They may be paid, but they were far more than employees. They were a big, happy family.

Taking care not to get in the way or hinder anyone's progress, Ellie cast a discerning eye over the preparations. She was glad to see they had placed the tables under the sprawling branches of the magnificent cedars, as she and Arnold had agreed. The shade would be welcome later. Coming to one of the already operational barbecue pits, she noted the bored youngster as he dutifully rotated the spit. The corners of her mouth and eyes lifted as she recalled how younger children, including herself once upon a time, considered it a privilege, a grown up privilege, to be allowed to turn the spit. Each soon learnt it didn't provide the expected fun, and how tedious a task it could be. Glancing into the ever brightening sky, she saw there was yet plenty of time. Arnold appeared to have everything under control, so she could afford to give the poor soul a brief break. His beaming face and straitening of back and shoulders, dejectedly bent beforehand, obviated any need for a verbal response. The grasp of a handy pillar prevented any disaster as, in his enthusiasm, he rushed past her. Calling out to his retreating back to return in half-an-hour, he acknowledged with a high wave of his hand. He then disappeared round the side of the large barn, from which she could hear the voices of children laughing and playing.

Appreciating the awning the men had erected over the pit, realising its shelter would be needed once the blazing sun had risen to its highest point, Ellie mindlessly rotated the spit as her thoughts returned to the past. It'd been some years since they'd last done this. Neither she nor her father had been up to entertaining people. They'd thought they never would be again. However, both eventually realised how unhappy it'd make Mummy if they didn't carry on with it. She'd cared about the people and had always sought ways to make life more pleasant. It would sadden her for it not to continue. Both struggled at first, but after deep heartfelt discussions knew it was what darling Mummy would want. Years! Felt more like centuries! As the deepening etchings on father's face attested. But, here they were, once again hopefully delighting the local populace. Under her mother's caring, watchful eye, this had become one of the most anticipated events of the year. Most villagers, and many from the surrounding district would attend. Though people had been careful not to be insensitive, or to cause upset or offence, it'd been clear how much they missed the occasion. She recalled how she herself had enjoyed the celebrations, but then she'd not had any responsibility for any of it. Today was a very different matter. Again, she felt the weight. 'Please help me, Mummy.', another heartfelt, under-breath prayer.

She wiped the dripping water from her face and arms. The boy had returned on time, as promised. That was better. Now to get ready. Picking a more suitable dress, the green one with the sunflower design, she quickly glanced in the mirror, returning a loose strand of her auburn hair to its proper place. Her thoughts immediately returned to the times when she and Mummy would stand before the mirror together. She could see it in her mind's eye. Her mummy standing just behind her with her loving hands rested on her little shoulders. Why? Why? Brushing the tears away, she knew this wasn't the time for them. With such memories still occupying her, she descended the stairs, ready as she ever would be, to fulfil her duties. A confident, robust knock at the door made her jump. She'd almost tripped, but managed to clutch the balustrade in time. Everyone knew, on open days like this, there was never any need to knock. The door was always kept unlocked on these days. Or had it been so long? Her astonishment and surprise were further enhanced by the discovery of her uncle on the doorstep. He rarely visited and there'd been no expectation of seeing him today. While embracing him and kissing his cheek, she noticed her aunt standing a little back, next to a man she didn't recognise. She immediately went over and gave her a warm hug. Her visits were even rarer than her husbands. When finished, her aunt turned toward the young man and asked Ellie if she didn't recognise him. A shake of her head confirmed she didn't. 'Don't you recognise your own cousin?' Laughing as she asked. 'Goodness Daniel, I'm sorry, but it's been years.' They'd been very young when he and his family had moved. 'It has, but I still recognise that smile and those curls.' A faint tingling scurried through her belly. 'Excuse my manners.', recalling her responsibility as the woman of the house. 'Please come in. Daddy will be thrilled to see you. I'll fetch him in a moment.' Standing back to wave them into the entrance hall. 'No, no, dear.', Ellie's aunt noting her husband's glance toward the library, where he knew they kept the good cognac. That can definitely wait for later. 'Looks like you're ready to get things going. We can catch up with your father over lunch.' Bowing to her desire, Ellie led the way to the celebrations. They discovered a large gathering already assembled, prompting the customary greetings and inquiries. Aware that her duties as hostess obliged her to circulate, her uncle, aunt, and cousin left her to welcome the guests while they went to find her father. There'd been no mistaking when they had. The pleasurable tones of her father's exclamations ringing through.

As the afternoon progressed, red faces and damp patches attested the inevitable rise in temperature. Everyone gratefully moved to the shade of the large cedars under which lunch was to be enjoyed. The nicely chilled local wines and fresh spring water also helped alleviate the impact of the heat. Ellie, still busy with her hostess duties, was pleased to see her father, with his brother and family, settled round a table. Other than herself, they were the only family he had. She knew how much he missed his brother. They'd always been the best of pals when young. When responsibilities permitted, she would sweep by and drop a word or two into the conversation with a warm, gentle squeeze of one or the other's shoulder.

A fountain of warm breath parted the intense atmosphere as Ellie finally allowed herself to relax. Bright smiles and infectious, resounding laughter had filled the air all day. As the sea ebbs at its appointed time, so had her tension. A light touch to her tummy revealed it now soft and pliable. The tight knot nowhere to be found. Another silent prayer of gratitude penetrated the heavens, followed by a barely audible 'If only you were here'. A thought never far from her soul that day, but one she kept to herself. A quick flick banished her tears to the ground. 'Congratulations Ellie, you've done wonders.' 'Thank you Cathy. I hope Mummy will be pleased.' 'Of course she will be. You couldn't have made this any better.' 'I agree.' 'Thank you Rosemary. You're all too kind.' 'Nonsense, everyone is loving it. They, we, have all missed these gatherings. So good of you and your dad to continue with them.' Ellie couldn't help a slightly tearful smile. 'Sorry my dear, we didn't mean to upset you.' She dismissed their concern with a sweep of her hand. 'It's just brought back so many memories. But Daddy and I realised how unhappy Mummy would be if we had abandoned these events altogether. I'm just sorry you had to wait so long.' 'It was worth the wait. You really have done your mama proud.' Further congratulations and words of appreciation followed as people prepared for the evening's entertainment.

Ellie had got a group of the local musicians together, who now, in response to an almost imperceptible nod of her head, started up. Her primary responsibilities now fulfilled, she could relax. It was now just a matter of ensuring a steady supply of refreshments, and Arnold had that well in hand. With a much lighter step, she joined her gathered family, what there was of it. It was now just the five of them.

Hardly had she sat when Daniel stood and offered his hand, politely waiting for her to respond. A few moments to rest her tired feet would have been welcome, but how could she refuse that broad smile? Besides, she was still hostess. Taking a moment to inhale a breath of the evening air, she took a proper look. There hadn't really been time before. With his slightly twisted nose, broad mouth, and less than six foot slender frame, he was not classically handsome, and yet there was something about him. Recovering her manners, she gave him a smile and, resting her hand in his, allowed him to gently and politely lift her from her seat.

There was a rhythm in his body she hadn't expected. She could feel it spiralling through him. It demanded a cohesive response, to which she was well matched, though conscious it might be seen as too provocative for their society. The heavy tiredness in her legs and feet vanished as they spun round the dance floor. She gratefully noted others were equally engaged and therefore oblivious to how close Daniel held her. A closeness she was aware she shouldn't allow, but felt incapable of resisting. When the musicians struck up a slower, more intimate tune, Ellie regained her equilibrium and decided it time to rejoin their parents. 'Thank you Daniel. I must say you're a good dancer.' 'So are you.' 'Mummy wanted me to learn all the social graces.', shyly dismissing his compliment. 'It's more than that. You and the music are almost as one.' The glint in his eye bringing a rosy sheen to her cheeks.

'You two look great together.', her aunt beaming at them both.

It seemed no one wanted to leave, but in the end, some had started to wilt and decided to call it a day. Each parted with warm words of appreciation, especially telling Ellie what a fantastic job she'd done. 'Your mama would have been very proud.'

When the last guest departed, the five of them withdrew to the drawing room, where Ellie had had the foresight to have the cognac ready. A sigh of satisfaction as she sunk into the soothing softness of the sofa had the others again complimenting her on a successful day. Not waving it away this time, she thanked them, saying how grateful she was they'd enjoyed it. 'Such a shame we have to leave tomorrow. I suppose I should say today.' 'Do you have to, Uncle?', disappointed, 'I've hardly had any time with you.' 'I'm afraid so dear. The business won't run itself.' 'Never mind that for now. Let's enjoy a cognac, Brother.' Ellie's father pouring a generous measure of the golden liquid into each of the five waiting glasses.

'Please don't leave it so long again.', all standing by the open door. 'I agree. It's been far too long.' Ellie's father reinforcing his daughter's request. 'We're getting on. Who knows how much more time we have.' 'Daddy! Please.' The idea of losing him still too sore to contemplate. 'I'm sorry, dear, but it's the truth. It'd be a shame not to see more of each other before the inevitable.' Clapping him on the back, his brother countermanded with, 'Come on, we're not that old yet. But, you're right, it has been too long.' With that, he embraced his brother. Ellie and her aunt did likewise and then each their respective in-law and relative. Unsure when it came to Daniel, she offered her hand, but he leant in and with a peck on her cheek bade her an, 'Au revoir, until we see each other again.', with an unmistakable twinkle in his eye. She smiled.

'There dear, I told you there was nothing to worry about. I knew you'd make it a success.' 'Do you really think it was, or were people just being kind?' 'Come on, you know as well as me when people are being genuine or false.' 'Yes, you're right. I hope Mummy could see.' 'I'm sure she could and will be very happy with what you achieved today.' 'I hope so.' 'Time for bed, I think. Not that there's much of the night left.' 'Goodnight Daddy.', kissing him with all the love she felt.

Sitting at her dressing table, watching as she brushed the tangled stands straight, Ellie thought back over the day. It had been a success, hadn't it? 'Thank you, Mummy.' Her thoughts then turned to the unexpected visit and the joy of having seen them. Daniel, in particular, unsure why he'd left such an impression.

2

TRADITION

As if a strong breeze was blowing her, Ellie's shoulders and neck perceptibly shifted, while her eyes remained focused on the altar screen. She wasn't about to let Brian know she could sense his annoying stare.

While she and her father chatted with family friends in the church courtyard afterward, he, along with others who'd shown more than a passing interest before, an interest she didn't share, made his continuing fascination more than obvious. As always, she didn't allow anyone to see she'd noticed. A deep breath helped subdue the burning desire to go straight up and confront them with unmistakable language. Of course, that'd never have done. It would've shocked the villagers to witness what they'd consider a brazen act. Why did men have to be so thick? Why couldn't they see she wasn't interested? Or could they and were just being bloody minded? Conscious she needed to keep her temper under control she, with a quick surreptitious head shake, banished the thoughts from her mind. When the conversations were over, she demurely walked beside her father, ensuring to keep her eyes averted.

Unbeknown to his daughter, Ellie's father was becoming increasingly concerned, sensing how things were changing within his own body. It was time to take action before it was too late. Broaching the subject, he knew, wouldn't be easy, but felt it had to be done sooner than later. He decided today would be a good opportunity.

Ellie smiled at her father while pouring the boiling water into the pot, little knowing what was coming. Though she was aware there seemed to be something on his mind. Placing the pot on the table, she gratefully sat, and they both silently watched the escaping steam as it rose from the spout. 'Ellie dear, we need to talk about your future.' 'What do you mean, Daddy?'. The faint shadow of a cloud crossing her features. 'I'll not be around forever dear.' 'Are you ill?', sitting straight. 'No, but time is marching on. We have to face the inevitable.' 'You've plenty more years yet.' 'We all have to go sometime.' 'I know.', struggling to hold back her rising tears, 'Mummy went far too early. It would be too unfair if you did as well.' 'I'm hardly young anymore. Not like your mama was.' 'Why did she have to go so early?' 'One of life's mysteries. It's said the good go early. Your mama was certainly one of the good ones.' 'Yes', remembering how loving and kind her mother had been to all. No one was ever turned away. Most who arrived in sorrow or pain had left with a smile and restored hope.

After a few minutes silence during which each was lost in their own thoughts, 'What do you mean by "my future"? My place is here with you, and always will be.' 'But, when I've gone?' 'Please stop saying that, Daddy.' 'We need to think about it, dear. You'll need someone to take control of the estates.' His meaning now becoming clear. 'Are you talking about marriage?', her face reddening. 'Yes, dear.' 'Why? Why do I need a man to run things? I'm as capable as any man. Better than many.' 'You are, but it's not right for a woman to do man's work.' 'You really can be old-fashioned sometimes.' 'I suppose so, but the old ways have worked well for generations.' 'Have they? Do you think women are happier living in a male dominated society, not being allowed to show their potential or capabilities? And, worse still, losing all rights to their own property and inheritance?' 'Your mama was happy. We both were.' 'You loved each other deeply. What you're proposing is an expedient marriage. One to satisfy society's expectations. I don't want that. If I marry, I want it to be for love, just like you. Can you imagine a lifetime tied to someone you didn't really care for, or they for you?' He'd expected some retaliation, but had forgotten how determined and independent she could be.

For a moment he sat silent, eyes cast to the flagstone floor. His enduring love and concern however, quickly revitalised him.

'You know more than one has approached me?' 'Yes, I'm aware.' 'Brian seems a nice chap.' Determined to pursue the topic as much as he could. 'Most of them are, on the surface.' 'Well?' 'Brian's a bore. He's incapable of making up his mind about anything.' 'Seems to have settled on you.' 'Only because he hasn't the wit to look elsewhere.' 'What about James? He's from a good family and would certainly be capable of running the estate.' 'The only person James is interested in, is himself. He thinks the world revolves round him and his wants. He couldn't give a damn about anyone, or anything else. Excuse my language, but of all people, he's one of the most frustrating I know. I know you're trying to do your best for me, and have been great at keeping the fortune hunters at bay. But, I don't see why I should be forced into a marriage I don't want, or need.' 'You don't want to be on your own forever, do you?' 'I have you. I'm happy. Why would I want anyone, or anything else? Of course, I'd love to have Mummy with us, but that can never be now.' 'No.' Time stopped for a moment as her father recalled the image of his beloved wife. He missed her as much as Ellie, maybe more. 'I appreciate I'm beginning to sound like a broken gramophone, but I will not be around forever. I don't want to leave you alone or unprotected.' 'I wish you'd stop talking like that, Daddy. You're not going anywhere soon. Besides, I'm more than capable of looking after myself. And, don't forget we have the staff. You know they're more family than anything else. They'd always help, if I ever need it.' 'I know, but it's not the same.'

Understanding fully he was just concerned for her welfare, she rose, bent, and gave him a kiss on the head. 'I need to see Arnold. He's some ideas for the top fields.' 'I also better be getting on.', appreciating there was nothing further to be gained from their conversation, for today at least. 'Okay then. I should be home in plenty of time for dinner. How does hotpot sound?' 'Lovely, you're just as good a cook as your mama.' 'Compliments indeed. We both know that's not strictly true, but thank you.'

Her tightening hamstrings brought her to the realisation she'd entered on the steep path leading to the top fields. She'd been preoccupied with thoughts revolving round the conversation she'd just had with her father. She knew as the daughter of a well-to-do family, there were conventions and protocols people expected her to adhere to. But why should she? Why could people not accept a woman can be as capable as a man? That they could run a business and make it a success. She knew full well her father was simply concerned about who would look after and protect her. He'd always done it and wanted to ensure there'd be someone after him. Tears rose again at the thought of them not being together. True, as the only child, they'd to be careful of fortune hunters. She was heir to a vast fortune. But her daddy had seen them off. What would happen when he was not around clearly troubled him. She knew that. His answer was the traditional solution of a husband. He was old-fashioned, and she had to accept that as well. But they'd been running the estates together for a long time and he knew she was more than capable. Why could that not be enough? Why did it always have to boil down to this for a woman? It wasn't right or fair. And it didn't help that many women adhered to the principle.

Finally reaching the fields, she pushed it all to the back of her mind. Arnold, the estate manager, outlined his proposal for changing the crops they grew in these fields. 'Our saffron crocuses aren't producing much these days. I suggest we turn these fields over to barley.' 'We'd lose a lot of revenue.' 'Sorry, didn't explain properly. I'm not suggesting we stop growing the crocuses. It's just we've been growing them here for a while and I think it's time they had fresh soil. We could turn the lower pasture over to them. The soil up here is still okay for barley.' Casting her eyes over the magnificent view of the fertile valley below them, Ellie took a moment to dig into the agricultural knowledge she'd gained over the years. Something about Arnold's idea was troubling her. What was it? Her eyes expanded as she recalled. 'Isn't the pasture too damp for them? The bulbs will rot. Won't they?' 'The pasture has good drainage, so there shouldn't be a problem. And it's always dry in summer, which will be good for them.' She took a moment to reflect on his reasoning, wanting to ensure they didn't make a mistake just for expediency. Concluding it would be the right decision and save them from losing revenue she confirmed her agreement. 'Okay Arnold, sounds good. I'd hate to loss the income from the saffron, besides which I love to use it myself. Will the barley bring in much?' 'Not as much, but should be adequate, provided we plant the right variety. It's a robust crop, so it should become a regular contributor.' 'Okay, I'll leave it to you then.', turning to head back down the steep incline.

'Hmm.' Turning back she noted his shifting feet and slightly embarrassed look. 'Something else Arnold?' 'Well, yes. I wasn't sure whether to bring it up with you or your father.' 'What is it?', noting how awkward he was obviously feeling, 'You know Daddy's left most of the estate administration to me these days.' 'Well, um.', quite out of character for him who was normally confidently sure of himself. 'Is something wrong? You know you can talk to me.' Stretching to his full six-foot-two height, he bit the bullet. 'Your uncle has asked me to work for him.' Stunned, Ellie stood as if her feet had suddenly rooted, while also looking him straight in the eye. The thought of Arnold not being around had never occurred. Though her father and she saw to the business side, it was mostly Arnold who oversaw the day to day running of the estate and management of the crops. In the same manner as a salmon jumps up cascading water, she sensed the streak of anger darting through. How could her uncle do such a thing? He must be aware of how much they relied on Arnold and of how long he'd been with them. 'I'm sorry Miss, I didn't want to upset you, but something had to be said. I...' 'Are you going to accept?', interrupting before he'd a chance to say more. 'It's not as bad as you may think. His manager has been with them since he was a boy and is now getting on a bit. Apparently, he's starting to find the work a bit too much.' 'He must've been training someone to take over?', her frustration getting the better of her. 'He has, but they're not ready to take full responsibility. Your uncle asked if I'd work part time for him, with the other half of my time being here. He's offered a very generous salary, considering it'd only be part time.' 'You're interested then?' 'I admit I am. I'd like to help your uncle and especially Bernard. He's the manager. We've been friends for years. I learnt a lot of what I know from him. He was a pseudo father to me when mine passed away. I was thinking, as you've learnt so much, and are more than capable of managing the estate, we could handle things between us. Naturally, I'd expect a reduction in pay.' Ellie now felt annoyed with herself for not having let him finish before reacting. 'I see. I'll talk it over with Daddy, but if you're determined, we can't stop you.' 'It's not like that, Miss. I'd never thought of working anywhere else. This is my home and where I belong. It's just I want to help Bernard. It'd be a way of repaying him for all his kindness to me. I'd still consider this my primary position.' Strained face and bent, rounded shoulders attested his genuine concern. 'It's all right, Arnold. I'm not cross with you, but uncle should have said something to us. It was wrong of him not to.' 'I'm sorry Miss, I'd thought he had but when neither of you said anything I began to wonder. That's why I brought it up today. I need to let him know what I'm going to do.' 'I rather think the decision's been made. Of course, you must help your friend. We'll just have to sort out how it's going to work. Don't worry about your pay, we won't cut it. You've been good to us and have done wonders with the crops. Anyway, you know you're more family than an employee.' 'Kind of you to say so Miss.' 'Come to the house this evening and we'll work something out between us.' 'Thank you Miss.' Each then went their own way. Arnold to get some of the hands to help prepare the pasture. Ellie to share the unexpected news with her father.

'Do you know if Daddy's in, Doris?' 'He's with a guest in the drawing room.' 'Guest?' 'Old Mrs Winkle. She called in just after lunch.' 'Thank you Doris.' Standing before the hall mirror, she ran her palms across the fabric of her dress and quickly repositioned some loose strands. 'Hello dear. Do you remember Mrs Winkle? Her husband, rest his soul, was an old friend.' 'Hello Daddy.', bending to kiss his cheek. 'Yes, of course. How are you Mrs Winkle?' 'A bit creaky these days, but otherwise not too bad.' 'How did you get on with Arnold dear?' 'Fine, we can talk about it later. We don't want to bore Mrs Winkle with business talk.' 'That's all right, dear, I was used to my husband always prattling on about the estate, this crop, that crop, new farming initiatives, and so on.' Bestowing a benevolent smile, as only those of her age could to someone so much younger. 'Kind of you, but it can wait.' The light clinking of teacups announced Doris's arrival with afternoon tea. 'When are we going to hear wedding bells then dear?', with a meaningful smile as Ellie poured the tea, 'I'm sure there must be a young man somewhere.' 'No, there's not.' 'But dear, you're of an age. You shouldn't leave it any longer. You don't want to end up a spinster.' She was on the edge of screaming when a stern look and a shake of head from her father brought her to her senses. 'Kind of you to be concerned, but no there's no one at present.' 'Really, I'm sure your mother would have had it sorted, if she were here. It's your responsibility now.' Giving Ellie's father a hard stare. With a smile that he hoped would pacify the old lady, he responded, 'You know what young people are like these days. There's always time.' As much as he wanted Ellie to marry, he wasn't going to allow her to be bullied. Anyway, he knew where that would likely lead. 'But there isn't, as you and I both know. Anyway, what will people think and, more to the point, what'll happen to the estate after you're gone?' This was too much. 'I'm quite capable of managing the estate.' 'That's not woman's work. You should be concentrating on having a family and keeping a home.' Knowing it unwise to pursue the matter further, and not wishing to upset their guest or her father, Ellie simply gave a side nod and smiled. Respect for her elders was something her mother had drummed into her, even if she thought them wrong. Her father came to the rescue by asking Mrs Winkle for what news she had. He knew she wouldn't be able to resist sharing what she'd heard.

'There dear, you see what people are already saying.' Mrs Winkle had just left. 'It's so narrow minded. You'd think a woman would appreciate someone trying to break the restrictive mould we're forced into. But, on the contrary, many of them actually hamper any possibility of progress. It's as if they're brainwashed.' 'People don't understand, dear. Remember, we're primarily a rural society. People have accepted the old ways for generations and, as I said earlier, they've worked. I do understand what you're saying, but I'm worried. If you carry on you're likely to find yourself ostracised, and alone. I honestly think you should marry.' 'I know, Daddy, but I'm not going to just marry anyone to keep other people happy. I don't want to upset you, but do you really want me to compromise on something I feel so strongly about? You know I'd never be happy with such an arrangement. If I marry, I want to have what you and Mummy have, had.' All four shoulders slumped at the mention of their loss. 'Hem, hem.', her father clearing his throat a few seconds later, 'You're determined? Silly question. I can't pretend not to be worried but, though I may not be able to stop myself mentioning it from time to time, I'll not press you anymore.' 'Thank you, Daddy. I just want us to live happily as we are. Should I ever fall in love, then who knows, but I doubt it'll ever happen.' Her father looked into her eyes with what seemed a sense of sadness before nodding in acceptance.

'Now, what news from Arnold? What plans has he for the top fields?' 'Oh, I almost forgot with all this talk of marriage. He suggested we move the saffron crop to the pasture and give the top fields over to barley. He thinks, because we've grown the crocuses there for so long, the land is no longer suitable. We discussed it for a while, and I think it makes sense. What do you think?' 'I agree, it does make sense. I'd started to think we should move them. The barley won't be so valuable, but it'll bring some money in. Better than leaving the fields idle.' 'There's something else. Did uncle say anything to you about his estate manager?' 'No, why?' She then explained all Arnold had told her. 'Really? Why didn't my brother say anything?' 'I don't know. I must admit it made me cross. Arnold is coming this evening so we can discuss it.' Her father sat silent for a few seconds and then, after evidently having reached a conclusion, continued, 'We could make it work, I suppose. If I take over the bookkeeping, you could oversee the estate when he's away.' 'We considered that, and I think we'd be able to make it work.' 'Good. We'll discuss the finer details this evening. In the meantime, I'll write to my brother and ask why he'd not discussed the matter with me first.' 'Try not to be too angry with him.' 'I won't be, but he needs to explain.' 'All right then Daddy, I'll leave you to it. Just need to check a couple of things in the barn before dinner.'

3

ARRIVAL

'Hello Daniel.' Surprised to find him in the library with her father. 'This is a pleasant surprise. Must be at least eighteen months since we saw you.' 'Twenty.' 'Really.', unsettled by the unexpected ripples in her tummy. 'I was telling him it's been far too long.' The beam on her father's face evidencing how pleased he was to see his nephew. 'Aren't your parents with you?', looking round in case she'd missed them sitting on the other sofa. 'No, I'm on my own this time.', giving her a warm smile that sent further ripples through her, 'Your father tells me you're overseeing most of the estate now.' 'Yes, I've just been down at what was the pasture. I wanted to see how our saffron crocuses like it there. This will be the first year we can expect a full crop.', hoping he hadn't noticed the slight blush she'd been unable to stop. 'I'm sorry about your estate manager. Dad didn't tell us he'd asked him to work for us as well. If he had, I would've told him to speak to your father first.' 'That would have been appreciated, but it seems to work. He still spends a lot of time here and I'm able to manage when he's not about. He's not too far away, should anything urgent arise, which thankfully, it hasn't so far.' 'I should be able to help with that, a little.' 'What do you mean?' 'I'm moving back.' Her father and she couldn't help their astonished stare. 'Ha, ha, no need to be so surprised.' 'We thought you were all settled in the city. What about your father's business?' 'City life doesn't really suit me. I've tried, more for mum and dad's sake than my own, but it's not working. I'm more of a country guy. I may have been young when we moved, but I've never forgotten. I belong here, in the rural wilderness, as some of my friends call it.' Ellie and her father remained sitting with slightly shocked expressions, still unable to master their surprise. Daniel smiled, and continued, 'I've decided to set up a practice in the village. I've got my doctor's degree and finished my internment with a city practice.' 'Oh.', neither being able to say more. 'I've bought the old bakery.' 'But it's a wreck.', regaining some of her composure. 'That doesn't matter. It's the land I want. It's nice and central. I'm going to build a surgery on it.' 'This is a surprise Daniel, my boy. What does your father say about it?' 'Wasn't too happy at first. But, thankfully, he's someone who listens. I told him how I'd been feeling about city life, and how much I missed our home here.' 'That must've surprised him.' 'Yes, and no. I think he'd been noticing for a while how unsettled I am.' 'I know my brother, he'd want you to take over the business at some stage.' 'Again, I think he realises I don't really have that much interest in it. My brother is more into it than me. He'll make a great managing director and has the wherewithal to make it a continuing success. I'd probably just drive it into the ground.' 'I'm sure that's not true.' 'Perhaps an exaggeration, but I honestly am not interested. Helping people is my forte. And looking after God's own earth.' 'My brother must be disappointed.' 'If he hadn't my brother, I think he would've put his foot down. As it is, he's given me his blessing, though made clear he'd have preferred it if I stayed. Anyway, it's not as if I'm moving to the other side of the world. I'll be living in the old family home and we'd see each other when he comes down. I'll also be helping Bernard with the estate, so that should free up some time for your man. We won't be able to do without him altogether, I'll have the practice to take care of. But that won't take all my time.' 'Thank you my boy. You're very thoughtful. Be good to have a doctor in the village again. There's not been one since old Mr Franks died.' Daniel responded with a shy smile.

'Well, that's a turn up for the books.' 'Indeed, it is Daddy. Who would ever have thought. I was sure we'd never see any of them living here again. After the excitement of the city, this must feel a very dull place.' 'Just goes to show, not everything is as people make out. The grass is never really any greener on the other side.' 'Ha, ha.' 'And it's not always greener on this side either.' His meaning ever clear. 'Now Daddy, you promised.' 'I said I'd try. We both know I'm not going to stop all together.' 'You also know I'm not about to change my mind.' 'I know, dear, but let an old man try.' She gave him a mischievous smile as she went to check on the dinner preparations.

Later, alone in her room, Ellie tried to make sense of what she was experiencing. Annoying, uncontrollable twitching, sensations of liquidation and then of ignition, a mind that wouldn't stay focused. It reminded her of when she'd been excited as a little girl. Throughout was the incomprehensible, persisting image of Daniel. Why? Perhaps it was the unexpected surprise of his coming to live in the village. To have another relative close by would be wonderful. She'd expected, eventually, still unable to comprehend her father not being there, she'd be the only one left. Now there was someone else to keep the family name and history alive. That must be it. With that satisfaction, she went to bed and slept through, undisturbed, to dawn.

4

AWAKENING

'I'm just going to the cafe Ellie.' 'That's good. You've not been all week. They'll be wondering where you are.' 'It's been a busy old time.' 'I'm sorry you've had to work so hard on the books. It's not what I intended when arranging matters with Arnold.' 'No worry, dear. I don't mind.' 'Thank you Daddy. Now, you take as much time as you want and enjoy yourself.' 'Thank you dear. I'll be back in time for lunch.' 'Okay.'

'You're looking peaky.' He'd just taken his seat at his usual table overlooking the village's main junction. Being on the corner and slightly raised, the cafe's terrace offered a good all round view of the village centre. 'Just the heat. It's hotter than usual. There's no real shelter on the way down.' His long-time friend eyed him with a doubtful look, but decided not to say more. 'How's that lovely daughter of yours?' 'Fine, busy, but fine.' 'I've heard she's taken on more now that your estate manager is also working for your brother.' 'Yes, she was actually quite keen to do so. She's learnt so much over the years and is very capable.' 'Still it's not really woman's work. It's about time she married.' 'I know, but Ellie's her own woman.' 'You know my son Richard is rather smitten with her?' 'Is he. No, I didn't know.' 'How about it then? Why don't we agree it between us? He'd be more than capable of running your estate.' 'As I said, Ellie's her own woman. She's made clear, if she marries, it'll be by her choice and to whom she chooses.' 'Bit unconventional.' 'I know, but that's how it is. Don't think I've not tried to persuade her otherwise. However, she's determined, if it happens, it'll be by her choosing.' 'What do you mean "if"? You can't mean she's willing to be a spinster?' 'Indeed, if it comes to it. She has made her mind up and that's the way it is.' 'You can't allow that. You should make her marry.' 'As said, I've tried but she's who she is, and quite frankly I love her for it.' 'People won't understand. She'll be ridiculed and excluded from society.' 'Doesn't seem to bother her.' 'Well, I never. Just imagine if all the girls decided to do the same.' Ellie's father shrugged his shoulders and, with a slight tilt of the head, implied they'd have to accept it.

'Are you all right, Daddy? You're not looking too good.' 'It's rather hot today and I've just come back up the hill. I'll be okay in a moment.' 'Are you sure? I've not seen you look so pale before.' 'No need to fuss, dear. I'll just a sit down before lunch, that's all I need.', letting out a deep breath as he gratefully lowered himself into a chair. After lunch, he'd been more than ready for a siesta.

'Good morning Sir.' 'Good morning my boy. We've not seen you for a while.' It was the next morning and he'd just sat to enjoy his mid-morning coffee on the front terrace. 'I've been busy getting the surgery fitted out. It's almost done, and I thought you and my cousin may like to have first look.' 'That would be nice. I'll get Ellie', starting to rise from his seat. 'Please don't trouble yourself.', noting the old man's exertion, 'I can call her. Do you know where she is?' 'In the kitchen.', gratefully lowering himself back into his seat.

'This is amazing, Daniel.' They were standing on the main village road before what was now the largest building in it. It towered a full one and a half stories above its nearest rival. 'It's like something out of the history books.' 'I got a taste for classical architecture in the city museums. I used to spend hours looking round them.' 'That explains all those marvellous statues and the balustrades round the top. But I have to say, it gives more the impression of a wealthy home than a surgery.' 'I didn't want to build anything boring. I know it may appear incongruous for here, but why not? Why should something functional not also be beautiful?' 'You've certainly achieved that. That gorgeous light blue sets those marble adornments off to perfection.' 'Come and have a look inside.' Ellie's father couldn't help but stop mid-step as they entered the vestibule. Further statues were scattered around, but what grabbed the eye was the amazing sweep of the gleaming white marble staircase as it wound up to the next floor. Not only that, but it was also so comfortably cool, negating the intense heat they'd been enduring outside. 'My boy, this is remarkable.' 'Thank you Sir. Must admit I'm very pleased with it. Let's go up. The consulting and treatment rooms are all on the next floor.' With all the latest equipment installed, these were impressive and reassuring rooms. They'd certainly make patients feel confident of receiving quality care. Daniel then took them onto the roof terrace where they could lean on the marble balustrades and absorb the breathtaking views across the valley in one direction, and of the village and forests nestled into the hillside in the other. While taking in the aspect of the fertile valley with the backdrop of purple hued mountains Ellie asked, 'When you look on this how can anyone say there's no God?' 'I know', Daniel's deeply held sincerity of faith more than evident in his voice, 'I can't imagine a life without Him in it.' 'No. I may not always understand, but I know He's true and fair, though it's difficult to see it sometimes.', thinking back to the loss of her mother. 'Are you all right, Sir?', a note of alarm in Daniel's voice. Ellie's father had just slumped onto one of the statues. 'Just the heat. I better go back in.' 'I'll check your blood pressure.' 'No need to fuss. I'll be okay in a minute.' Daniel gave Ellie a doubtful glance. Between them, they got her father back in and into one of the treatment rooms. 'Please don't bother yourself, my boy. I'll be okay in a moment.' 'No bother, Sir. As we're here, I might as well check.' 'Is something wrong Daniel?', noting the concern in his eyes, which he'd tried to conceal. 'Your father's blood pressure is a little high.' 'Just the heat, as I said, my boy. Nothing to worry about. I'll soon be over it.' 'We better get you home where you can rest. I think I may need to carry out some further tests over the next days. You're not looking too good.' 'Please don't fuss. I'll be okay.'

~~~~~~~~~~

'I'm so sorry Ellie. There was nothing I could do.' 'I don't understand. Except for that little turn the other day, he was fine. I was sure he'd go on for many more years.' 'Truth is, he hadn't been telling you everything. When I examined him, I found signs that his heart had been troubling him. When I asked, he said there'd been a couple of "tweaks", to use his word, it was nothing. You know what he was like. I tried to get him to tell me more, but he just told me not to fuss and to let him rest. I knew I wouldn't get any more out of him that day, but had decided I wasn't going to leave it there.' 'Could you have done anything?' 'I think it was too late. His age was also against us. I would've tried a couple of therapies. If nothing else, they may've made him more comfortable. But, the Lord

37

had other ideas. To be honest, I think it was his time.' 'It wasn't mine.', feeling annoyed with her Lord, 'I know I shouldn't talk like that, but He'd already taken Mummy. Couldn't He let me have Daddy for a while longer?' 'It's not our place to question The Lord. He knows best.' 'I know but ...', tears now streaming. 'Would you like me to speak to the priest?' 'No!', anger getting the better of her, 'Sorry, that was a bit abrupt. Thank you, but I'll sort it. Daddy has always said how he wants to be with Mummy when his time came. He often talked to the priest about it. In some ways, I think he resented having to wait. If it hadn't been for his love for me, I think he'd have given up long ago. They really loved each other.' 'I understand. I'm here if you need me. For anything.' 'Thank you Daniel.'

The sight of her mother's open grave, ready to accept her father's coffin, nearly brought her to her knees. She grabbed Daniel's arm to steady herself. In the midst, she found herself surprised by how firm and muscular it was. The final lowering of the terrible box into the shadowy pit proved her breaking point. Her tears, which had been a steady flow, now became a torrent. She let go of Daniel's arm, and falling on her knees, went to grab the coffin. This couldn't be happening. It was wrong. It hadn't been his time. The agonising, confusing thoughts whirling through her. Daniel only just managed to save her from falling in. Gently lifting her to her feet, he let her lean on him and allowed her tears to soak through his shirt.

'Thank you Doris, and please also thank everyone else. I'm not up to it at the moment.' 'Of course, Miss. I'm so sorry.', wiping tears from her own eyes. 'He was a major part of all our lives.', placing a grateful hand on Doris's arm. 'Feels like I've lost my own father.' 'I know dear.' 'Sorry Miss, shouldn't be bothering you like this.' 'It's all right Doris. I understand.' 'Thank you Miss.' Having thanked the last of the mourners and seeing them out, Ellie went to the drawing room, feeling the need for its peace in the evening dimness. Automatically, she moved to the French doors that, since her mother's passing, had become her quiet place. She found the view across the beautifully kept lawn to the evergreens and beyond soothing. Here she could let her tears fall unrestrained, no longer needing to be aware of other people's needs.

'Hmm, hmm.' Her spine and hips nearly dislocated as she spun round. 'Sorry Ellie, I didn't mean to frighten you.' 'Oh, it's only you.' 'Charming.' 'I didn't mean it like that. It's just I'm glad I don't have to pretend I'm okay.' 'I know. I'm sorry, I should know better. This isn't a time for levity.' She gave him a warm, grateful smile, appreciating his understanding. Moving to her side, he placed an arm round her shoulders and then let her lean back against his toned muscular chest. They stood silently, gazing through the glass.

With a gasp, Ellie clutched her abdomen as a painful surge of grief and sorrow shot through. Turning, she clasped his shoulders for support and sank her face into his chest. A cascading waterfall of tears followed. He held her close as the bitter reverberations also entered his soul. They were as one.

As the tears subsided, Ellie looked up into his gentle brown eyes. He looked back into hers. He bent and kissed her full on the mouth. She responded and then lay her head back on his chest. A half hour passed with neither moving nor speaking. It then dawned on Ellie what they'd just done. How could she do such a thing, at such a time? Pulling back, she struggled to comprehend. Putting space between them by shifting back into the room, she battled the intensifying confusion, the unexpected attraction, her embarrassment, and above all, the guilt. At such a moment, it was wrong. At any moment, it would be wrong. What would people say if they saw? More, what would her parents think? She shook her head, trying to clear the thoughts and banish the sensuous delight his lips had left. This was not the time. It never could or would be. She dared not turn, not sure how she would act if she looked at him again.

Daniel, sensing and understanding the confusion he saw playing out before him, remained still and quiet. It was certainly not the best timing, but he'd been unable to resist. She'd looked so vulnerable and in need. He had to comfort her, though, if he was to be honest with himself, he'd wanted to kiss her for a long time. Guilt and fear also rose in him now, as he witnessed the devastation his lack of self control had led to. To hurt her was the very last thing he wanted. 'You okay?' Silence followed. 'I'm sorry. I didn't mean to upset you.' He then berated himself for his stupidity. 'I think you better go.', but at the same time looking over her shoulder and directly into his eyes, unmistakable passion all too evident in her own lustrous green eyes. As he looked into them, he felt his soul being drawn from him as if to make them as one. He knew, however, it wasn't the time to act upon it.

She returned to the window, where she remained with torn heart and confused emotions until dusk drew its curtain across the scene. 'You should have something to eat Miss.' 'I'm not hungry, thank you Doris.' 'I'm sorry Miss, we're all going to miss him.' 'Yes, we are.' 'Are you sure you won't have something? Something light?' 'Thank you Doris, but I really couldn't stomach anything. I'll just stay here for a little longer and then go to bed. You and the others can retire now. I'll take care of myself.' 'As long as you're sure Miss?' 'I am, thank you.' 'Goodnight then Miss.' 'Goodnight Doris.'

5

GUILT

With lead weighted legs, bent shoulders and lowered head, Ellie trudged her way to the top fields. It was all so wrong. Her Daddy should be here, he should be having a say in the decisions. It wasn't right for her to do this without him. Wet patches exploding on the dry, dusty surface beneath her feet marked her path. To now have to live without the two of them was too much. 'Why Lord? Why? Why couldn't you spare them for a little longer?' Her constant inner questioning, always followed by the guilt of having questioned her Lord. Recurring thoughts of Daniel didn't help. They would have been troubling at any time, but now! When not questioning her Lord, she'd ask herself why these thoughts of Danial crowded in. She didn't want them, the little girl within her cried. She wanted to be with her Mummy and Daddy, that was all, nothing more. They belonged together. They were never supposed to be apart. She longed to hear their voices. To speak with them. To hug them again. Tears flowed with the power of a rampaging river, soaking the front of her dress. Stopping to rest beneath an old cypress, she tried to swallow the burning bile. She needed to get her head clear. There were decisions to be made and, like it or not, she had to make them.

'Good morning Miss.' 'Good morning Arnold. Thank you for meeting me here.' 'No trouble Miss.', noting her dejected drawn looks and tear-streaked face, 'How may I help?', deciding it'd be unfair to intrude into her sorrow. Inwardly shaking herself, Ellie struggled to concentrate. 'I wanted to ask if you think we should continue with the barley. It's not been producing very much.' 'True Miss. I've also been thinking about it. I suggest for the next year or two we allow the land to lie fallow. It's been in constant use for many years and would benefit from being left idle for a while.', glancing back across the field to confirm his thoughts. 'I agree. Let's do that then.' 'Very well Miss, I'll get it sorted.' 'Thank you Arnold. I really don't know what I would've done without you these last months.' 'I'm only too glad to have been able to help. Your cousin taking over some of the bookkeeping and management has lessened the time I need to spend with Bernard. Means I can again spend the bulk of my time looking after things here. They still need me some of the time, but it's not that demanding.' 'As long as you're sure. If they do need you, please give them all the time required. I don't want them to have any problems because of me.' 'That's nice of you, Miss. But they seem to have things under control. As I say, I still spend some time with them, so am able to put my two pennies worth in when necessary.' 'How's my cousin? I haven't seen him for a while?' 'Seems well enough, Miss. People in the village are grateful for him. He's apparently helped many, at least that's what I hear.' 'That's good.', she was pleased to learn he'd been accepted back into village society, 'I'll leave you to it then Arnold.' 'Thank you, Miss. Please remember I'm always available if you need me.', confirming it with a look of genuine care and by adding 'for whatever.' 'Thank you.' Turning to retrace her steps, she first took a moment to look across the familiar valley, but the joy in it was no longer there. Tears returned. As she had since her father's passing, she forced herself to get on, knowing there was no one else. It was hard, but she couldn't let her Daddy down. He'd worked hard to make the business a success and would be sad if she let it go.

~~~~~~~~~~

From the dim shadows at the rear of the nave, Daniel watched the fidgeting figure.

Sorrow, confusion, embarrassment, shame, and guilt interweaved. Why, at such a time, when her mind and thoughts should be focusing on her Lord, was she seeing images of her mother, father, and Daniel swimming round? Mother and father perhaps made sense, but Daniel? She felt her face redden, causing her to pull the headscarf closer. Daniel's heart went out.

Grateful for the service's end, Ellie moved with the throng into the brilliant sunshine. Obligatory greetings exchanged, she was ready to head home when a familiar voice stopped her mid-track. 'Daniel! What a surprise. I haven't seen you in church for some time.' 'No. Thought it better I stay away for a while, and I've been visiting my folks.' 'How are they?', manifestly sidestepping the first part of his statement. 'Well, thank you.' 'They must miss you.' 'In some ways I suppose, but definitely not from the business side of things. My brother's in his element, as I said he would be. Dad's given him a greater part in running things and he's loving it. Apparently, he's already secured some new contracts. I'd have been hopeless at it.' 'I'm sure that's not true.' He smiled his appreciation for her trust in his capabilities. 'May I walk you home? Be nice to catch up a little.' 'Um,' shifting from one foot to the other, 'thank you, that'd be nice.' Concluding no harm could come from it. As they were going down the church steps, Ellie stumbled, her foot having caught in the hem of her dress. Daniel immediately extended his muscular arm to support her. An involuntary blush came as she took his hand. 'Thank you.' 'You're not right yet, are you?' 'It's nothing, my foot caught on my hem.' 'That's not what I mean, and you know it.' His familiarity made her uncomfortable.

'Really Daniel, I'm alright.', said a little sharply. She didn't want anyone feeling sorry for her. Daniel understood and wanted to make amends quickly; 'I'm sorry. I didn't mean to offend you. I'm just concerned. You're not looking yourself, and I noticed how unsettled you were in church.' A further blush rose with the realisation someone had noticed. 'I still can't get used to attending a service on my own. We always came as a family, and now...,' her words trailing off. 'It must be hard, but people say it gets easier with time.' 'I doubt it. I force myself to do things round the estate because I know they'd be upset and maybe even cross if I didn't. But, it's really for them.' 'I'm sorry Ellie.' Instinctively going to give her a hug, but quickly thinking better of it, pushed his hands into his pockets. 'How are you getting on with your own estates?', purposely changing the subject. 'Fine, your Arnold has been a Godsend. He really knows his stuff.' 'Yes, we've been fortunate to have him with us all these years. Daddy and he met at one of the agricultural events and became instant friends. He tells me your own manager is getting on a bit and isn't able to do as much as he used to anymore.' 'Yes, it's sad to see Bernard struggling so. He's been with us since he was a boy. His father used to work for grandad. I think their family has been on the land for almost as long as ours.' 'Arnold told me you've taken on a lot of the work yourself.' 'Yes, thought I might as well learn while Bernard's still here and your man can spare us some time. I realise it was a bit of an imposition, Dad asking him to help us, but we would've struggled without him.' 'I admit I was a bit cross he hadn't spoken to Daddy first, but it's been okay. I'd already learnt a lot and had been doing a fair proportion of the work for a while, despite Daddy not considering it work for a woman. He could be old-fashioned at times. Anyway, now you've taken part of the burden, Arnold says he can spend a lot more time caring for our estate.' 'Shame I can't let you have him back full time yet. I've the surgery to see to as well.' 'I wondered how you'd manage.' 'Can be tiring sometimes but thankfully I love both. Anyway, it won't be forever. Bernard's been training one of our capable younger boys. I say boy but he's now eighteen and has been shadowing Bernard for sometime. Bernard says he has a keen mind, is very observant, and asks a lot of questions. He's already taking on more responsibility.' 'That's good. I was concerned you may be burning the candle at both ends, so to speak.' 'Ha, ha, suppose I was for a while.' Charmed by the thought of her being concerned for him.

'Here we are. Thank you for walking me home.' Daniel's half smile couldn't hide the disappointment he felt with this apparent dismissal. Ellie hesitated. She'd relaxed during the walk, having forgotten what pleasant company he was. Uncertainty grasped her, but she thought twice. After all, he was her cousin. 'Would you like to stay for lunch? Doris is bound to have cooked far more than we need.' The upturned corners of his mouth said it all. 'That's kind of you. If you're sure?' 'Of course. Come on in.'

'That was sumptuous.', tapping his full belly, 'Why don't you come up to mine tomorrow and I'll show you round?' 'I'd like that. I've never been to your estate. Silly really, considering how close our properties are and that we're family.' 'We left when you and I were quite young, so there hasn't been occasion for you to come up.'

~~~~~~~~~~

'I had no idea your home was so beautiful.' Daniel had shown her round the entire house, and they were now back in the elegant drawing room, with its unique green and gold embossed wall paper and complementing green velvet, gold trimmed seating. 'Grandad loved the best of everything. He was determined his home would mimic a stately one. He must have been better off than I realised. Mind, costs were far more realistic in those days, though this must've still cost a pretty penny.' 'Must take a lot to maintain it.' 'Actually no. Besides style and luxury, grandad insisted on quality. Only the best would do. As a consequence, the building has withstood the ravages of many winters and summers fairly well. We still have the original roof.' 'Goodness.' 'We occasionally have to tidy up a bit of paintwork or repair a minor nick, where someone has been careless, but other than that, there's nothing much.' 'That's remarkable. Most houses this size need constant maintenance. I know ours does.' Daniel smiled and with a slight upward side motion of his head and eyes confirmed he was aware of the fact, but grateful his home wasn't one of those. 'Enough of this place, let me show you the rest.' With that, he opened the door and waited for her to exit before him. 'The barns are like any barn, so I'll not bother with those for now. What I want to show you are the cottages. Few people know we have them.' With a nod, he indicated they should go up the slope and into the copse adorning the rise. 'This is lovely Daniel.' They were standing in the centre of the sentinel pine trees, taking in the view their elevated spot granted them. The spread canopy of interlocking branches provided a welcome respite from the sun's burning rays. 'I used to love playing cowboys in here. Dad would hide behind one of the trees, though with his build they never concealed him.' 'Ha, ha, he is a substantial man.' Daniel was pleased to see her laughing again, even if it was momentary.

'The cottages are just over that rise.', pointing to a further hillock a couple of hundred metres beyond the copse. 'These are pretty. Doesn't anyone live in them?', noting their unkempt condition. 'Not anymore. We used to let our retired workers see out their days in them. But, many have now opted for having their own houses in the village that they can pass on to their children.' 'Sad to see such lovely places left to decay.' 'I make sure that doesn't happen. They're part of my heritage and who knows, someone like Bernard may like to live in one when he retires. He's not got his own family and precious few other relatives.' 'That's really considerate.' 'Ah.', brushing away the compliment with a sweep of his hand, 'there's one more place I'd like to show you.' 'More!' 'Just one, but a special one. You may need to take my hand. The path's a bit rough.' Without thinking, she accepted his proffered support. A tingling immediately ran up her arm and into her torso. Not an unpleasant sensation, but one that almost had her withdrawing her hand. However, she kept a firm grip, using the uneven path he'd not exaggerated about to justify it to herself. 'Goodness, this is beautiful. Who lived here?' Before them stood an impressive, double bay, two-story house. She couldn't bring herself to think of it as a cottage. 'You know back in grandad's time, people saw any disability as a curse or punishment.' 'Yes, it was terrible.' 'And, you also know anyone seen to associate with any such person brought condemnation upon themselves?' 'Yes.', said with a quizzical look, as it was obvious there was more to come. 'Well, what no one outside the family knows is grandad had a disabled child. His legs were twisted, and he had fits. Grandad didn't want him exposed to the ignorance of people, so he built this house for him. He lived here his whole life with no one, except the family, knowing.' 'Poor thing. Must've been lonely.' 'Grandad ensured he wasn't. He employed a confidential nurse and three staff to care for him. They were all sworn to secrecy.' 'Grandma and Grandad would visit regularly. They loved him very much and spent a lot of time playing with him. From what I understand, he was a bright, cheerful boy. He's buried in the garden. He died when he was fifteen.' 'That's so sad.' 'It is, but at least they made his brief life as happy as they could. The house is still in good order. Would you like to see?' 'If you're sure I won't be intruding.' 'It's okay. I never knew him, so, though I feel sorry, I don't have any actual emotional connection.'

The interior didn't disappoint. The best furniture from the period filled the space and, despite the dust, the gilded finishes still held their sparkle. 'My goodness, they certainly made this a lovely home for him.' 'They did. Again, no expense was spared. The rest of the place is just as impressive.' 'And you say no one outside the family knows of its existence?' 'No, except for Bernard. He was a boy himself at the time. He would help carry wood and food up. He's never told anyone. Amazing for a boy of his age, but he's always been trustworthy.' While talking, he noticed Ellie's eyes had drifted to the further corner of the hall, where a door with a small cross on it stood. 'Like to see inside?' 'Oh, sorry. That was rude of me.' 'Not at all. I can see you're intrigued.' 'Well, yes, I am.' Striding across, Daniel opened the door and, with a nod, invited her to enter.

'This is beautiful.' 'They couldn't take their son to church with them, so built this chapel. My grandparents would come here after morning service. They'd then share a family worship time together. They were very devout and, so I've been told, was he, despite his limitations.' 'Something that runs in the family.', giving him a straight, slightly raised eyebrow look. 'You've noticed. Yes, I believe strongly in our Lord. And ours is not the only family to share our beliefs.', his turn to look straight at her. 'Yes.' Shyly turning away to look at some images that had been carefully placed above the little altar. 'Let's have a look upstairs.', deciding it time to move on. Six bedrooms opened up from the central landing. 'Each person had their own room. Quite something at the time, as most servants had to share. This is the main bedroom.', opening the largest door. Dominating the room was an elegant four poster with gold fringed, deep blue velvet curtains surrounding it. An equally elegant walnut washstand stood in the bay still supporting its beautifully decorated porcelain washbowl and jug. 'What an attractive room. And, what a fantastic view.' She was standing beside the washstand, looking through the slightly grimy window.

His hand on her shoulder made her jump. 'Ellie dear, I've tried but I've got to tell you how I feel.' The loving look in his eyes diminishing her initial intent to move she turned back to the window. 'I think you realised a long time ago,

I'm in love with you.' Fear, confusion, embarrassment, guilt, and other emotional turbulence spun in her mind, heart, and abdomen. She'd been fighting hard to subdue her feelings, and now, with a few simple words, he'd demolished all her efforts. Focusing on the magnificent redwood opposite, she waited for the spinning to settle. All the time his breath tickled her earlobe. The beating turbulence finally calming, she turned back to face him. Her intended words stuck as she looked into those eyes again. Resistance failed as she sunk into him. Sensing the change, he lifted her chin and kissed her. All residual resistance evaporated. She responded.

After ten minutes so entwined, her conscious reasserted itself. Alongside it, a sudden nauseating, confusing sea swirled. Accusing fingers of guilt, shame, and fear dug their sharp nails into her. She must put a stop to it! She mustn't let it go further, no matter how much she wanted it. Gently pushing him away, she slid from his arms and fled to the door. 'No Daniel, this is wrong.' 'Why?' 'We're cousins, first cousins!' 'Why should that matter? We're told God is love and what's more pure than true love?' 'But God can't approve of this.' 'I suspect it's not God you're thinking of but people.' 'I'm not that shallow! However, now that you've brought it up, you know we could never live free together. The church, let alone people, would ostracise us, or worse. You know how they are about things like this.' 'All that aside, are you honestly telling me you don't feel the same?' She could no longer look at him with assurance. With eyes fixed on the carpet, her feet shifted uncomfortably. 'I think I better go.' 'I didn't want to upset you but we've to face facts. It's now up to you. I love you, but I'll not force you into anything.' 'Thank you.', barely audible above her beating heart. To her, at least. 'I'll walk you back.' Her only response, a nod of acceptance. She made a point of keeping a physical distance between them as they wound their way through the trees and then down the hill, willing to risk the possibility of her tripping without his support. When back at the house, she made clear she would make her own way home. Daniel, a little bewildered, stood by his door and watched her retreating figure. His heart ached to hold her again, but he was a man of his word. It now had to be her decision.

Her emotions in total turmoil, she nearly stumbled several times, her blurred vision making it difficult to see the pits and stony obstacles. This had been so unexpected. She'd never thought love would be hers, now certain it was love she had and felt for Daniel. A life of comparative solitude and spinsterhood had been her expectation. It would still have to be. There was no way the two of them could be together, even if she'd been prepared to chance it. God wouldn't approve, nor would her parents. No, it had to be this way. If it had to happen, why could it not have been with someone else? They were first cousins! It'd never do!

Over the following weeks, she concentrated on running the business and ensuring all the staff were provided and cared for. Each morning she had to banish the guilt, shame, embarrassment, and confusion, and do her best to calm the inner trembling. Yet, she remained unsettled, though, through her strength of character and self-discipline, managed to hide it from all but herself. Each day she prayed for forgiveness, as if she'd intentionally fallen in love with her own cousin. But even The Lord's compassion couldn't penetrate her sense of guilt. Her heart, spirit, and soul remained in torment. She ached for the love she'd now become aware could be hers, but also feared it. It was wrong, wrong, wrong. She'd throw herself into the business and estate and banish thoughts of Daniel and love. She'd follow her mother's example and spend her remaining time caring for the poor and needy. That was what her life would and had to be about. All thoughts of such a love had to be dismissed, bared, and expelled. It could not, and must never, be allowed. It had to end here and now. It must not be thought of again.

6

DANIEL

'What's the point?' Daniel was standing in the centre of his new surgery, taking in the splendour he'd created. But, instead of satisfaction, he felt the cold emptiness of futility. Why had he bothered? What had all his hard work been for? He'd expected to have children to inherit it. Children with someone he loved. What was so wrong about his love? It was genuine, sincere, boundless, and true. Who the hell had said it was wrong? Who had the right? Why were people so condemning? Hypocrites! He knew from what many had shared in their moments of need, when he was treating them, how many had things to hide. How if the truth came out they'd be denounced and rejected. And yet, they were prepared to censure others. Frustration, anger, indignation, irritation, and resentment tightened their grip round his lungs, forcing the oxygen out. He tried to inhale, but the little breath he could muster caught in his throat. He needed air. He needed to breathe.

On the roof terrace, he leaned against a statue of Aphrodite, and recalled the moment he and Ellie had stood close, enjoying the panorama. How good it'd felt to be in such close proximity. To have sensed the vitality within her. To have imbibed the aroma of her person. A moment when he'd longed to touch her, to embrace her, and to show her the depth of his love. It'd been a surprise to him how he'd fallen so quickly for her. To have so suddenly experienced a love so deep it hurt. He'd never suspected love could be so intense, so all-consuming. Nor how hard it would be to hold back, to observe convention, and to subdue a beating heart. A tear accompanied his rising pain. He'd previously ridiculed the thought of someone having a broken heart. Now he knew better.

God said love is good. The bible says love comes from God, and that anyone who does not love does not know God. So how can it be so wrong? How can anyone consider it an evil? Why was it so difficult to love? He clutched at his head, almost tearing hair from its roots. He had to stifle the rising anguish that was searching for an exit. It wouldn't do to give anyone a hint of what he was enduring and why. They'd never understand, and it would compromise Ellie, even though she was the innocent party. He didn't want that. It was all him. He'd been the one to force the point. He'd been the one who'd seduced her into an action she wouldn't have otherwise entertained. No, no one must know. He must get himself under control. If anything was to happen, if there was any chance of them moving forward together, it would have to be at her choosing. But at what cost? And, if she didn't choose?

He allowed the tear to drop, and then those that had been queuing to follow. At least he was out of sight and hearing. Anger, self-recrimination, and regret enveloped him. Wrapping round him like some sodden woollen cloak, ready to stifle and suffocate, the weight of it all tangible as he lambasted himself. He shouldn't have put her in that position. He shouldn't have been so weak. He was a man! Self-control was an ability he'd always been proud of. Why had he allowed himself to be so undermined? So weak? Love, it was love. Damned love! It wasn't supposed to be difficult to love. At least not like this. Love was supposed to be happy, joyful, precious. He clutched his chest and took deep breaths to calm his raggedly beating heart. The pain finally subsided with further intakes until he was able to regain some control. Shifting his shoulders, as if trying to throw off a heavy load, he stood straight and gazed across the panorama. The same one they'd enjoyed together. How different and less appealing it seemed now, though he wasn't really seeing it, a mind mist having descended across his eyes. Not seeing the lush valley dotted with its variety of smallholdings, nor the brilliance of the blue and white crystal dance as the river flowed across rocks. The purple grey mountains rising on the further side as if the spine of some gigantic monolithic monster also eluded him. All sights she'd delightedly pointed out. It was a view that normally drew a sigh of contentment and thanksgiving. Not today. Instead, his mind rebelling, a variety of desirable scenarios played through, all of which he knew within his depths were unlikely to find fruition. Grasping, as so often troubled souls do, he argued within his unsettled mind the conclusion wasn't a forgone. There is always hope. Where would we be without it? More settled. More stable. His logical side argued back. The chimes of the church clock, but a couple of metres across the road, reverberated through his comatose frame, awaking him to the fact it was time to open the surgery door. Whatever his own condition, his patients needed attending. It would be wrong to allow them to suffer because of his own self-pity.

He tried to listen to his clients' woes and sorrows, but in his distracted state, most of it went from one ear to the other, passing into the ether unchanged, unchallenged. Did his patients notice? Probably not, too absorbed with their own concerns to contemplate what someone else may be enduring.

Surgery completed, he returned to the terrace and statue of Aphrodite. Was this to be the end of all his hopes? Would he have to hold his love a secret for the rest of his days? Could he? For her sake, he'd have to. But could he?

How long he stood there he'd no idea. It wasn't until the shadows of dusk began to dim the light he realised it must have been hours. He should move and go home. But he didn't want to leave the spot where they'd been together. Where he'd felt the full impact of his love. Where he could still see her form. Reaching out, his hand met the cold, unresponsive marble of the statue, and not the soft, delicate flesh he'd expected. The cold, unrelenting hardness reawakened him. He attempted to clear his mind with a shake of his head, but the diffused vision wouldn't leave. Slumping back, he embraced the statue and allowed the tears to flow unrestrained. Again he clasped his chest. Such pain. Such sorrow. The bitter taste in his mouth mirrored that in his soul. Looking up for a moment, he saw dusk had now left and the darkness of night cloaked everything before him. But he remained, unresponsive to the night air, the owls cries, or the jabbering insects. If this was to be the end of his hope, his love, then this would be where he belonged. Where he'd take his last breath. The mirage of her form stood before him again, though to him it was no mirage. It was real. It was true. Again he reached out, only to be disappointed as before. This time, not only the cold marble but also the cooling night finally penetrating, he looked about him as if bewildered, uncertain of where he was. Then, realising, he disentangled himself from the statue's support. His staff would wonder where he was. As with his patients, he couldn't afford to give them any hint of what was going on. He'd better get back.

Unable to look life in the face, he made his way home with cast down eyes and hunched shoulders until reaching his door. He stood silently on the doorstep looking back to where the valley would be, though darkness hid it from sight. Further tears were ready to flow, but he forced them back. Again shifting his shoulders, he made himself stand straight. They mustn't see the state he was in. He had to protect her, no matter the cost to himself. He'd have to pretend, though to be false went against everything he believed. But she was too precious. She mustn't be endangered or her reputation damaged. If anyone had to suffer, it would be him. He was the one at fault. It was all him, not her. But he knew no matter how much he'd say it, no one would understand or accept the fact. They'd be too ready to condemn, despite the guilty secrets many of them harboured within themselves.

7

DECISION

'Our reading today is from 1 Corinthians, chapter 13. *"Love is patient, love is kind, and is not jealous; love does not brag and is not arrogant, does not act unbecomingly; it does not seek its own, is not provoked, does not take into account a wrong suffered, does not rejoice in unrighteousness, but rejoices with the truth; bears all things, believes all things, hopes all things, endures all things. Love never fails."* Here we have the true definition of what love really is. Not the sentimental, insubstantial, thing so many talk of. That is not real love, if it may be called love at all. True love seeks the good of the other without demanding, or expecting, recompense. It willingly gives for the benefit of the other, no matter what.'

The jolt as her torso unilaterally shot toward the vaulted rafters took Ellie by surprise. It was as if solid black iron gates had suddenly swung open, allowing the full brilliance of heavenly light to rush out and inhabit all before it. The rest of the priest's words were lost to her. Her mind swirled with the realisation. What a fool! Of course, love was, as he'd said, a gift, a gift from the Lord. And, true love isn't selfish, it wants the good of the other. 'I want that for him. I want him to be happy. I want him to have joy in this life.', quietly announcing the truth to herself. She had to force her backside into the pew, resisting the temptation to rush out immediately. Glancing round, she checked whether anyone had noticed, conscious she'd been more than just fidgeting. Thankfully, her fellow congregants were attentive, eyes fixed upon the priest and ears attuned to his every word.

A service had never seemed so long before. At its end, she barely accommodated the polite social requirement to greet neighbours and friends. 'Control, control', she muttered within. It'd not do to rush away without a word. Besides being seen as rude, it'd be out of character and undoubtedly draw undesired attention. It may be a gift from God, but many wouldn't see it as such. They'd be aghast and condemnatory. Though generally a free spirit, she was also wise enough not to bring or provoke unnecessary censure. It wouldn't just be her. She also had to think of Daniel. To hurt him, or anyone, went against her heart and soul. No, she'd still have to be sensible. She'd have to keep her emotions under control.

'I'm so glad I caught you.' Turning to see who'd spoken, Ellie, despite wanting to get away as soon as she could, was pleased to see her friend. 'Hello Rosemary, you're looking well.', noting how chipper her friend was looking, 'Am I?' 'Yes.' 'Nice of you to say so. I'm so glad to have caught you.' 'Yes, you said. Why? Can I do something for you?' 'No, no. I just wanted to thank you again for the other day. It was great, you did such a marvellous job. I just wanted to make sure you know how much we all appreciated it.' 'Thank you, Rosemary, you said so on the evening, but I appreciate you telling me again.' 'There was a lot happening then and I really wanted to ensure you knew.' 'Thank you. By the way, did I notice you and Eric being rather friendly?' The sudden rosiness entering her friend's cheeks rather confirmed the matter with no need for words. 'Oh, you noticed.', blushing again. 'It was hard not to. Is there something going on I should know about?' 'Well,' hesitating for a moment, 'yes and no. I do like him, and I'm sure he likes me, but it's early days and I'd rather no one knew for a while. Not until I'm sure it's not just my imagination.' 'I can assure you, from the viewpoint I had, there's nothing imaginary about it. I'm so pleased for you. He's nice, and you'd make a great couple.' 'Thank you, Ellie, you've no idea what that means to me. I've always trusted your judgment.' 'Ahh.', brushing the compliment away with a wave of her hand. 'I better be going. The rest are looking a bit impatient. Anyway, thank you again for the other day, and for this.', the last bit quietly spoken with a shy smile. 'Please don't tell anyone, especially my brother. Since father died, he's become rather possessive and controlling. He doesn't like the idea of either of us seeing anyone. He's become obsessed with money and with keeping the estates together.' 'I'm sorry to hear that. But unless you ask me to, I won't tell him or anyone else.' 'Thank you. I know I can trust you.' Ellie simply smiled an acknowledgment of that truth.

Finally, sensing she'd done her duty to society and protocol, having ensured she'd also had a quick chat with a couple of other ladies, she bade farewell and headed off. Most would assume she was returning home. Little did they know. Once out of sight of those still lingering in the church courtyard, she darted onto the track that led to the higher parts of the village. She'd been surprised not to have seen Daniel at the service, knowing how deep his faith was.

Remembering he'd once said he liked to go to the secret cottage some Sunday afternoons, she decide to bypass the house and head straight there, though not entirely certain she'd recall the path. She needn't have been concerned. As they had that first time, she stopped in the midst of the copse, to catch her breath, calm her excited nerves, and take in the marvellous view across the open fields to the proud, rising foothills. They were truly privileged to live in such a beautiful area. No one could say it wasn't blessed by God. The quiet, calming surrounds having settled her agitation, she continued

66

her journey. As she cleared the next rise, the cottage's eves came into view. Her heart gave a little leap.

What if she'd made a mistake and he wasn't there? Should she go to the house? What about the servants? 'Don't be silly. It wouldn't be strange for me to visit. We're cousins!', she chided herself. What was that? A shadow? A glimpse of something passing behind what she knew had been the poor boy's bedroom window. She'd been right. Now assured he was there. With a light heart and a skip, she almost ran to the cottage door. Within a few seconds, her gentle knock had Daniel opening it. 'I've been such a fool.', her words tumbling out like some gigantic landslide, 'How could our love be anything but good.' With that, she fell onto his chest and embraced him tightly, feeling as if her life depended upon her not letting go. Taken completely by surprise, Daniel stood with wide eyes, and arms opened to each side of the figure now hugging his toned torso for all it was worth. It took a couple of moments before he realised what was happening. In a pincer movement, his arms curled round the precious treasure now attached to him. His mind whirled. Could it be true, or was his head in a far worse state than he'd realised? Was this just a mirage, or a daydream from which he'd wake any moment? Was any of it real? Her rapidly beating breast laying against his soon told him how real it all was. That it was the treasure of his life he held in his arms. How long they stood embraced on the doorstep neither could have told. To them, it was eternal. A moment not to be relinquished. Neither cared if they never moved again. This was what their lives were for. Both would've been happy if their Lord took them at that very moment. Nothing else mattered. Never would again. Each felt the intensity of the other's belief that they'd at last found the true fulfilment for their lives, their final destination on this earth.

With his head resting on her abdomen, she watched as the sun's rays, though dimmed by the grimy glass of the window, highlighted his gently rippling muscles and the rhythmic rise and fall of his broad shoulders. Caressing his raven locks, she allowed her breathing to return to its normal pace, though still anticipating his waking fully aroused. How could something that was so obviously right be so wrong? How could something so beautiful be thought evil or ugly? How could anyone consider their love anything but genuine? Anyway, even if she possessed an iota of inclination, which at that moment she didn't, resistance would have been futile. They belonged together, of that she was now sure. Her thoughts turned to when they'd been children, when there'd been no thought of such a possibility. Though they'd been very young, they'd always got on. Had there been something then? Perhaps a foreshadowing? Did such things happen? Who knew? The Lord alone knew what the future held.

Her thoughts then followed that train. What about their future now? She knew they'd never be able to be public about their relationship. It would always have to be hidden. A secret they'd have to guard all their lives. Would that be possible? Would they be able to hide it? It would be a struggle, a struggle they'd rather not endure, but what choice did they have? People would never understand. They'd be quickly denounced and spurned. She was fully aware, even her reputable family name and wealth would be no guard against that. It wouldn't be tolerated. First cousins in an intimate relationship! They'd be aghast. Though Daniel would understand, she wondered how willing he'd be to keep it quiet. Would he be willing? He cared as much as her about the villagers and she was sure wouldn't want to cause them upset, but he'd already argued about the rightness of their love. Would he feel it wrong to hide it? Would he want to shout it out?

8

INTERFERENCE

Ellie was pleased to find, as she entered the figures, indications were for it to be a successful year. The last barley harvest had payed its way better than expected. Daddy would've been so pleased. Her hand paused over the page as the memories and sorrow flooded back. It was hard to have lost them both long before she'd been ready. Would she have ever been ready? A knock at the front door broke her train of thought. She'd let Doris answer. Returning her attention to the bookkeeping, Ellie checked the invoice for the next figure to be entered. She noted how costs were going up, but thankfully, so had their income. Another knock, this time at the study door that she only kept closed when needing to concentrate, interrupted her thought processes again. 'Come in.' 'Sorry to trouble you when you're busy, Miss, but Mr George has called. I've put him in the drawing room.' 'Thank you Doris. I wonder what he wants.' 'He didn't say Miss.'

'Okay, I'll just put these away.', indicating the ledgers spread across the desk. 'Very well, Miss. I'll tell him you'll be along in a moment.' 'Thank you.'

'Good morning Mr George, this is a pleasant surprise.' 'Thought it about time I came. Been a while since your father's funeral.' 'Yes.' Unable to bring herself to say more for fear of embarrassing herself, 'Shall I ring for some tea?' 'No thanks, I'm fine, but you have some.' 'Thank you, but I won't just now.' He gave her a kindly, uncle type smile. 'I'll come straight to the point,' confirming what she'd suspected, that this wasn't just a courtesy visit, 'hum, sorry. I get a bit impatient at times. My wife is always telling me off about it. First, how are you?' 'I'm well, thank you.' 'Missing your father no doubt.' 'Very much. It was hard enough losing Mummy so early, but now to be without them both hurts.' 'I can understand that. You know your father and I have been friends for years, since we were young men.' 'Yes I do. He often talked about those early days and the things you used to get up to.' 'Oh dear. Ha, ha.' 'No need to worry. He was careful to only share the fun things, not that I would imagine you got up to any serious mischief.' His coughing and slight blush implied there'd been more than what she knew.

'I promised your father I'd look out for your welfare.' 'That was very kind.', she said politely but with inner irritation. 'He was concerned about what'd happen to you when he was no longer around.' 'He needn't have been. He knew full well I can look after myself.' 'And yet I see no sign of a husband.' Her temper immediately flared, staggered that someone not related would have the audacity to mention such a thing now she was on her own. She crossed to the window to calm herself, before she gave way and said something she'd regret. She didn't want to be rude. Turning back to face him, she simply uttered a 'No'. 'You need someone to run the estate.', promoting a further flash of temper. 'I'm quite capable of doing that myself, Mr George!' 'It's not woman's work. You should be concentrating on having a family. How else will your family's heritage continue? You're the last of this branch.' 'I'm fully aware of that. And as far as the estate is concerned, I'm as capable as any man. In fact, it's doing very well. I was working on the accounts before you came and the business is well in profit. So, I don't see the need for a man to run things.' 'Your father said you were an independent sort.' 'I expect he also told you about my attitude to marriage.' 'He did, very unconventional, but he was still worried.' Giving her a straight stare to emphasis the point. 'We talked about it, and he understood that, if I marry, it'll be at my choosing and to whom I choose. No one else!' 'It's not right. People will think you've gone mad. I've been checking out a few potential candidates .....' 'WHAT!' This was a step too far. Fearing she'd really lose control this time, she turned back to the window and took a deep breath. 'I'm only doing what your father should've long ago.' The silence, while she fought to rein in her temper, hung heavy in the air. Aware he may've touched a nerve and even perhaps overstepped the mark, Mr George sat quietly, waiting for the response he was sure would come. Too nervous to turn back yet, Ellie remained where she was, looking across the lawn to the misty foothills in the distance. The peaceful panoramic view finally penetrating into her soul, she turned back to face the audacious man. 'He did. As I said, we talked about it. He suggested a few possibles, but none were for me. Now, if you don't mind, we'll stop this conversation.' Still struggling to control the rage running rampant within. Her parent's teaching to treat elders with respect, something she'd always done before, helped calm her desire to be blunt and rude, though it was a battle. 'I was only trying to help. I gave my word to your father I'd look out for you, and that's what I'm trying to do.' 'I know, and I appreciate you mean well. But this is my life, and I wish to live it the way I want. Daddy understood that. He also knew I'm capable of running the estate and business. I was helping him do it long before he left. He was happy I could manage.' 'He was very proud of you. Often saying he didn't know how he'd cope without you.' 'Well then, surely that must satisfy you?' 'It's not right though. People don't expect a woman to run a business. They'll wonder what's wrong if you don't have a husband and family.' 'People may think what they like. I'm old enough, and wealthy enough, to make my own decisions. I will live my life as I see fit, not to please people.', this time giving him a very direct look to ensure he understood, and then added, 'And, in case you're worried about it, I'm not going to allow some fortune hunter to get the better of me.' 'I see you're determined. Your father told me you were, but I hadn't appreciated how strongly you felt. I apologise for clearly upsetting you. It wasn't my intention. I just want the best for you, or should say the best your father wanted for you.' 'I do understand, Mr George, but as you see, I don't need any help.' 'You are a remarkable woman, but I fear people won't understand. You may find, in time, life becoming difficult for you in the village.' 'Times are changing. Hopefully, perceptions will also change alongside. If not, I'll just have to live with it.' 'Well my dear, I've tried to do my duty.' 'I know. Daddy would be grateful. Please be assured he did understand, though always making clear he'd rather I followed convention. He also understood how I wasn't prepared to let convention and old-fashioned tradition govern me. Though reluctant to accept it, he also knew I'm an example of how women will make their own decisions in the future.' Though Mr George had his doubts about that, he decided not to say more on the subject. 'As I said, he truly was proud of you and often boasted how competent you are. He was right. I now see you are.' 'Thank you.' 'Well, it's time I was going. Apologies again for upsetting you.' 'I quite understand. Please don't let this stop you from calling in the future. I'd like us to remain friends. There are few who knew Daddy as you did. I'd love to hear more about what he, and you, got up to.' 'Ha, ha, not sure how wise that'd be. Good day, Miss Ellie.' 'Good day, Mr George.'

She watched his retreating back as he made his way down the hill, conscious she'd not been as gracious as she should've been. Why did people have to be so bound up with protocols and traditions? She then questioned, not for the first time, why she couldn't accept them as the other women did? But that's not who God had made her. It'd betray all she was meant to be if she acquiesced. Anyway, she didn't want to and whatever the consequences, she'd have to live with them.

Her thoughts then naturally transferred to Daniel. Mr George had been right about how people would view her single state. But, how much worse would it be if they ever found out about Daniel?

9

HIDDEN

'Hello Daniel. Unusual to see you shopping.' They were standing by the door of the local general store, each struggling to keep their hands from meeting. 'Hello cousin,' an unmistakable twinkle in his eye, 'we need some more disinfectant. Rachel's had to go to her aunt's in the city, so it's fallen to me to do the shopping today.' 'Is her aunt unwell?' 'Don't think so. Something to do with papers that need signing. Hope she won't be away for too long. Thanks for recommending her. She's been great. Couldn't ask for a better receptionist. Everyone loves her.' 'I'm so glad. We were at school together. It was sad when the job she loved was taken away.' 'How do you mean?' 'The firm she worked for got taken over and the new owners closed most of the district branches. They offered her a job at head office, but that's in the city. She couldn't leave her family, especially since her mother became so ill.' 'Sadly, there's little I can do for her. Even the newer painkillers aren't having much effect. It's really disappointing. She's such a lovely lady.'

'What you two being so serious about?' They'd not noticed the store keeper coming to the door. Instinctively, they jumped apart. Something their new companion didn't fail to notice. 'Oh', Daniel attempting to negate the guilty embarrassment he was foolishly feeling, 'hello Mr Ward. How are you keeping?' 'Fine Doctor, fine.' 'Good.' Daniel then remained silent while slightly nervously shifting his feet. A further thing Mr Ward didn't fail to note while he waited for Daniel's order. Realising one wasn't about to come, he asked, 'How may I help you?' 'Oh, yes. Thank you. We've run out of disinfectant. Two large bottles please.' 'Okay, and you Miss Ellie?' 'Thank you,' conscious she was also acting guiltily, 'I need some forest green cotton, if you've any.' 'But of course Miss Ellie. I do my best to keep a good stock for you and the other ladies.' 'Very kind of you, Mr Ward. Two reels if you have them, please.' Annoyed with herself for feeling as if caught in some childish prank. Having fulfilled each of the orders and accepting the payments, the store keeper stood by the door and quizzically watched as each headed in different directions. He, however, didn't miss the furtive wave each gave the other. With thumb and index finger, he stroked his chin.

Stretching full length across the crumpled sheets, Daniel reached out to caress her firm bosom. 'Daniel, we need to talk.

Seriously.' 'Now? I was just thinking how nice it'd be to stay like this forever.' 'A lovely thought, but not one we can ever hope to fulfil.' 'Why not?!' 'You know it's not possible. We're going to have to be careful. People can't know.' 'Why the hell not?!' 'Come on darling, don't get so worked up. You know they can't, they'd not understand, and you know what they're like when they don't.' 'But you've always been your own woman. Why let this change that?' 'I'm not. Though I don't believe in letting others dictate my life, there are times when it's best to be circumspect. It'd do no one any good to flout our love in the open. There's also my family name to consider and your doctor's practice. I know I don't like convention, but my parents are highly respected people and were both proud of our name. I'd hate to be the one to bring disrespect and shame upon it. And, you know as well as I do, your patients would probably drift away if they suspected some immoral goings on. You know how church doctrine rules many of their lives. I can't see the church condoning our relationship. Can you?' 'Damn it, I know you're right, but it's frustrating. Why can't people be allowed to live their lives the way they want? It's not as if either of us is married, though I wish we were.' 'Ha, ha. That really would be a step too far for most. Anyway, I doubt we'd be able to find a priest willing to marry us.' 'Who said I was talking of marrying you?' 'You beast.' Both unable to subdue their laughter or returning passion.

Turning from checking herself in the mirror, 'Remember darling, we've really got to be careful.' 'Damn it!' 'I know, but people really wouldn't understand and you know how quick they are to spot something different. I think Mr Ward was suspicious. We're going to have to be more careful.' 'Bloody man should mind his own business.' 'Don't be silly. We'd be the same.' 'Suppose so.' 'Don't sulk, it doesn't suit you.' 'When we going to see each other again?' 'Better give it a couple of days.' 'Are we going to have to live like this for the rest of our lives?' 'Unless church doctrine or society dramatically changes, yes.'

~~~~~~~~

'Good morning Miss. What time would you like lunch today?' 'I'll be out for lunch.' 'Oh.' 'Daniel's invited me over to his.' 'You going there a lot these days.' Irritation immediately rose. Doing her best to repress, and hopefully conceal it, Ellie responded 'He's my only relative now, well in the district at least.' 'Sorry Miss, I didn't mean to be rude.' 'It's okay Doris. I miss Mummy and Daddy and it's just nice to spend time with another member of the family, even if they're not a direct descendent.' 'I see that. Agnus was the same when her parents passed. She was forever visiting her aunt.' 'It helps bring some normality into our lives, though they can never be the same. Grief is a hard thing. Such visits help us deal with it.' 'Agnus used to say the same thing.'

'How do you explain to your staff the constant desire to have lunch at the cottage?' 'I don't. They're all aware of how I've always liked to spend time here and have just accepted it. They probably think I'm a bit eccentric. Perhaps I am, but it works in our favour.' 'But, don't they wonder about you asking for a picnic hamper?' 'I've never been a great eater, so they know a sandwich, tomato and fruit together with the small flask of wine is all I want. Talking of which I hope you're not too hungry. I couldn't ask them to make it for two.' 'No, far from it. Anyway, I'm not that keen on lunch. Breakfast and a light evening meal are usually more than enough for me.' 'Goody, more for me.' 'You greedy pig.', both laughingly collapsing into a bundled heap.

To avoid drawing undesirable attention, Daniel most often sat near the back of the church with one of his elderly patients. Everyone thought he was just being kind, as many of them were frail. Not entirely an untruth. He did care about them, but given the freedom to choose, he would've preferred to sit with the one he cared most about in this world. But he'd listened and knew full well Ellie was right. She usually was. Thankfully, they didn't have to be so circumspect after the service when congregants generally milled about, greeting their friends and neighbours. It'd have looked strange if they'd not spoken. Keeping their caressing eyes and hands from each other was, however, a strain. Often they had to make a point of turning to greet someone else to avoid their eyes lingering. There were several who were quite astute and rarely missed anything. Sadly, many of them also tended to be gossips. Once they started, it spread like wildfire, irrespective of whether it was true or false. No one seemed to care, preferring the enjoyment of the titivation it provided in their otherwise humdrum lives.

Unfortunately, their closeness was not missed by all. 'Ellie, my dear.' 'Oh, hello.', turning to find an old friend of her mother's standing just behind her, 'How are you Mrs Combs? It's been a while.' 'It has, my dear. I am well, thank you. I notice you and your cousin seem to have become very close.' A guilty blush rushed into her face before she could stop it. 'You know what it's like. I find his company comforting now I no longer have Daddy with me.' The deception made her sad, but she knew there was no other choice. 'Um, yes I suppose so.' Squeezing her eyes quizzically. Some doubt clearly in her mind. Sensing the need to reaffirm the point, Ellie continued, 'He's the only relative I have in the district and, though naturally it's not the same, he's in some ways a substitute for the man I love, loved, so much. I miss Daddy very much.', tears welling in her eyes. 'There, dear, do not upset yourself. Of course, you miss him and your mother, I presume.' 'Dreadfully. To have her taken so early has been very hard. We both felt it terribly, but having each other helped us both live with our loss. To now also be without him is too awful. I had hoped for a few more years together. He wasn't that old.' 'I am sorry dear, I may only imagine how hard it is. I can see how your cousin can be a comfort. He seems nice. I know many of his patients like him. I think some of them dote on him a little.' 'He is nice, and so sincere. He told me, whereas some look for a good income and the prestige, his purpose in becoming a doctor was solely to help people.' 'He is certainly doing that. I have not seen some of my friends with such a spring in their step since we were girls.' 'That's good to hear. He worries sometimes that he's not doing enough.' 'Well, you best tell him from me, he is doing more than enough. His patients are some of the healthiest I know. If that makes sense.' 'Ha, ha, yes, it does. Thank you, I will be sure to tell him. He'll be so pleased.' 'Good. I better be going. Some friends are coming over for lunch and I am going to be late if I am not careful. That would never do. You must come for lunch one day and bring your cousin with you. It would give me a chance to get to know him and learn more about his therapeutic ways. I have been with our doctor all my life, so will not be tempted to change, but it will be nice to see what has made my friends so perky. If you will excuse the expression.' 'Of course. Lunch would be lovely.' 'I will send a note when I have found a free slot. My husband's politics have quite overtaken our social calendar, but needs must. Though to be honest, I enjoy meeting such a variety of interesting people.'

'Are we in for a cross-examination?' Ellie had just told him about their lunch invite. 'I think we might be. I'm not sure she fully accepted my explanation for us spending time together. She's quite a wise old owl. Nothing usually gets past her, and even if it does, she normally finds out in the end. As many have discovered to their cost. She's not the most tolerant of people. We'll have to be super careful.' 'Can't even enjoy an afternoon out together.' 'I know darling, but it's the way it is. And though the circumstances may be different, we're not the only ones. Rosemary and Eric, for example. I know it's more to do with her greedy brother, but it must still be difficult. And who knows whether others are hiding something similar?' 'I know you're right, but it's still frustrating and shouldn't be necessary. People should be allowed to live their lives the way they want.' 'They should, but that's just not the way it is.' 'How about going away for a few days?' 'Lovely idea, but how could we explain it, especially as I've never been in the habit of going away? You'd be able to say you're visiting your parents, but me?' 'You could visit them too. After all, they're your relatives too.' 'And what would we tell them? It'd be just the same as being here.' 'We wouldn't have to go to them. Who'd know?' 'Dangerous idea. Suppose someone needs to contact us, you for your patients or me for the estate? And, what if your parents want to contact you?' 'Neither of those is a likely scenario, though I take your meaning. Be just our luck for something like that to happen.'

10

—— ⚬ ——

DAGGER

Though he'd tried his best to deny it to himself, he'd never been able to fully subjugate the sensation of sin. Despite the words and passages he'd quoted, he'd felt deep down they were breaking God's law. But then, was it God's or man's law? Was it more what the church demanded rather than the will of the Almighty?

'So we see any sexual intimacy between close relatives is wrong. Some try to argue, as God is love and their love is genuine, it must be okay. In other words, they cannot be sinning. If that were the case, why the punishment? Any children born from such an immoral relationship either die early or have a mental or physical condition. Surely that is God's punishment. You may find it incongruous that a loving God would punish His people. But all actions have a consequence, and in this case, it is as I have stated. There can be no escaping the eye of God.'

Daniel sat dumbfounded. It was as if a dagger had penetrated his heart. Had entered his very soul. Here was the confirmation, the condemnation, he'd been hoping to avoid, had hoped didn't exist. It now seemed his soul, or spirit, or whatever it was, had been telling him the truth. They were in sin. They were breaking God's law. There could be no escaping it now. Despite their love being genuine, it was wrong. It was SIN. He struggled to keep back the tears. She was his breath, his life. His existence made no sense without her. There could be no life for him unless she was in it.

His troubled thoughts occupied him to such an extent he almost missed the polite requirement for customary greetings following a service. His friends, patients, and acquaintances had to call to him twice to get his attention. 'Are you all right, Daniel? You look a bit off colour.' 'Um. Oh. Yes, sorry.', struggling to think what he could say and hoping they'd not notice his inner trembling. 'Just a bit tired, sorry.' 'I hope you are not overdoing it. People have little concept of a doctor ever being off duty.' 'No, nothing like that. I just found it stuffy last night and couldn't really sleep.' 'It was a bit close. Must be a storm brewing somewhere.' 'Perhaps. Please excuse me, but I think I'll go home and try to have a nap before lunch.' 'Good idea. Now you take care. We cannot have you going ill. Anyway, who would take care of you. Ha, ha.' 'Indeed. Thank you for your kindness. Good Day.'

The fact he reached his own home at all that afternoon was a surprise. His meandering footsteps could have led him anywhere. He'd not noticed. His sensations of guilt and sin were now added to with thoughts of what he'd say to Ellie, and of where their lives would lead after. Dark, depressing, invasive, painful anguish and fear took hold as he contemplated the possibilities. The idea of parting was anathema for him. How could he go on living without her? There was no life without her. There was no breath without her. There could never be anything without her. It would be the end of everything for him. The thought then struck that she'd not been at the service, which was unusual for her. She wasn't ill, was she? No, of course not. She'd have come to him, or sent a note for him to go to her. As her doctor.

Ellie had stayed home to help with one of the horses that'd taken ill during the night. He was a prized stallion she'd grown up with and loved dearly. For reasons she couldn't explain, it clearly not being anything to do with the immediate worry, she'd felt unsettled. Daniel had flashed in her mind more than once and she began to wonder if something was wrong with him. He'd been less than his confident, assured self recently. She knew, despite his words, how deep down, he felt uncertain about their relationship in the eyes of their Lord. And yet, he knew as well as she did, they belonged together. They both felt it. How strange life can be. She'd been the one to first run from the idea, believing it to be sinful. He'd been the one confident it must be right, arguing how could such genuine love, the depth of theirs, be anything but right. How God was love and their love must therefore be born of Him. And now it was her confidently stating they belonged together and him with the doubts. Perhaps she was just tired after sitting up half the night. It was probably all her imagination. He'd be fine and the old confident self when they next saw each other.

As he'd told his friend at the church, so he told his servants. He was tired and was going to lie down for a while. He'd skip lunch. None questioned him because they could see how pale and drawn he was. Tiredness seemed the obvious answer. They knew how much he put into the practice and into taking care of his patients, as well as the estate. Along with most of the village, they admired his commitment and genuine caring. They were truly lucky to have a doctor like him.

His unsettled spirit stopped him from resting. He tried laying down in the cool of his room but rebounding thunderclaps of anguish and anxiety kept him twisting from one side to the other. Rather like a snake that has been bitten by a predator. Striding round the room or slumping on the sofa proved no better. His soul and spirit rebelled against what he'd heard. He couldn't accept it. He wouldn't! There, mind made up. But that was all a deception. God could see. His Lord knew the truth. What to do? What to do? Life without her .... 'Dear Lord, is that what you really want?'

Continuing despondent thoughts and worries kept him from sleeping that night, and shrouded all in the day following. Was this really it? Was there no hope? Wasn't there some way round it? Each question brought a resounding NO. A no that reverberated within his heart, throughout his soul, and in his conscience. Despite feeling, or perhaps hoping, that was more his own reasoning than the Lord's, he knew their relationship was a dangerous one. Dangerous on this earth for sure with the likelihood of condemnation and rejection if discovered. But, of more concern was the possibility of it leading to neither of them being allowed into their Lord's presence. He didn't want either for Ellie, and would prefer not to have to face either himself. He clasped his head and twisted about in anguish as fear rose with greater force than it had before. It was hopeless. They were trapped. Whatever he, they, did it would be wrong. To part would destroy him. To live would be too painful. There was, could be, no future without her. There could be no life unless it was with her. He couldn't live on this earth without her. Was this what The Lord really wanted? For them to be apart, though still on the same planet? Was there no way through? Was there nothing he could do?

In his desperate search for an answer, the idea struck that they could go away. That would deal with the condemnation, criticism and rejection, but they could never escape the eye of God. Wherever they may go, He would always see. Anyway, he knew Ellie wouldn't want to live like that, and he had to accept nor would he. He also knew she wouldn't want to leave the home and estate her parents had built, and which she now maintained for their sake. She'd feel it'd be a betrayal of their trust and love. What to do? What to do? The constant question running through every pore and nerve. The one question that needed an answer. The one question to which he could find no answer. Or, did he know the answer, but was unwilling to accept it? Was he trying to persuade their Lord it wasn't wrong? That because their love was genuine, it was okay. To grant them a blessing, to condone and say all was well, even if it wasn't. Or was it okay and just the rules of men that were driving his fevered fear? That possibility raised his hope, but second thoughts brought him back to the worry of it being him trying to deceive himself. 'Dear Lord, what are we to do? Is this what you really want? Our separation? Our parting? For us to no longer, to never, be together?' He clutched at his heart, his consternation seeming to have brought it to a stop.

11

CONFUSION

'I can't believe that's what The Lord really wants. And yet, I suppose I can see it.' Daniel's evident torment pulled her heartstrings. 'What's changed your mind?' 'What the priest said.' 'And you think he's right?' 'He's supposed to know God's mind, or at least what's in the Bible, which is assumed to be how Our Lord lets us know His mind.' 'What happened to God is Love and our love must therefore be from Him?' 'I don't know!' 'No need to be testy, I'm just trying to understand. It was me who first thought it was wrong but then realised how our love fulfils the ethos of what the Bible tells us about love in 1 Corinthians.' 'I know, I know.' Turning to the window and bewilderedly gazing out on to God's wondrous creation. To look at her and know it may be the last time they could be so private and personal was proving too much for him.

'Darling, what is it you're really trying to say?' He remained by the window, shifting his feet one way, then another. The strain in his features drawing her heart further. But she knew to go and embrace him at this moment would be wrong. He needed to make clear his thoughts and feelings on his own initiative, without any intimate distraction. 'I don't know. Or do I? Yes, I suppose I do.' Again, agitatedly shifting his feet about, 'I think', stopping to take a deep breath while pressing his hand against his stomach, 'The Lord wants us to stop.' The deep breath of just a moment ago now left. His shoulders slumped in unison with the resulting deflation. 'Stop seeing each other, you mean?' 'Yes.' Still gazing out of the window, though no longer seeing what was before him, and still unable to look at her. 'Is that what you really want?' Shock had him spinning round, disconcerted she'd even asked. 'Of course Not!' 'Okay, okay. I understand. But, despite what you and I both feel, and know, you think we must stop?' 'Yes.' Visibly twitching from head to toe, his agitation having now taken full control. 'Daniel, you know how much I love you and, though it would be difficult and break my heart, I'm willing to do whatever you consider is for the best.', unable to stop the tear in her eye. 'I know. You're such a treasure.' 'I hope I'm more than that.' 'You know what I mean.' A slight smile finally crossing his features, if only briefly.

'Why don't we leave it overnight? Perhaps it'll be clearer after a good night's rest.' 'That's not a likely scenario. Sleep? As if I could. Why does the Bible have to be so paradoxical? Our love is genuine and we do want the best for each other. Why isn't that sufficient? What's it matter if we are related? Why should it make any difference?' 'I don't know. If, if, it's what God is saying and not the interpretation of men, I'd also like to know why. I'm aware of the possible consequences, the so-called punishment, but are those a condemnation or just one of those inexplicable life events, of which there're many?' He could see and understood it was a genuine question and not an attempt to justify their love, the way he had frequently done since hearing the priest's words. 'I wish I knew. The priest seemed certain they're a punishment but, like you, I'm not sure. But, all that aside, what're we to do? I don't want us to part and I'm not sure if I could handle it if we did. You're everything to me. You're my life. I can't imagine a life without you by my side.' He dejectedly hung his head, unable to hold back his frustrated tears any longer. Sensing he'd now said all he could, Ellie embraced him, allowing all the love she had for him to flow. She lifted his chin and, looking into his eyes, saw the anguish within his soul. An anguish that mirrored her own.

12

COPSE

'Mr Bernard says come quick Miss! It's the Master!' Ellie recognised the young man Daniel's estate manager was training to take over from him. Before she could ask, he'd run back down the path. The urgency in his voice left no room for hesitation. Within seconds, she was running down the path after him.

Out of breath, she couldn't ask, but one servant pointed up to where the cottages were. His strained face gave rise to deep fear and, though she could've done with catching her breath, she was off again at an even faster pace. The further up the hill she got, and the more the copse came into view, the further her fear escalated. She could see several people milling about.

Finally reaching the outer edge of the copse, she hesitated. Something was seriously wrong. Spotting her, Bernard immediately came over and, with deeply drawn eyes, shook his head. 'I'm sorry Miss.' 'What do you mean Bernard?'

In response, he just turned his head forty-five degrees and stared. Ellie followed his sight line and nearly collapsed. On the ground, between the legs of the milling men, lay something covered with an old jacket. 'No, no, no.' Almost inaudible. Reaching a hand out to support her, Bernard led the way. There was now no mistaking the human form that lay beneath the jacket. She stared with disbelief and then turned questioning eyes to her companion. Without a word, he lifted his eyes up. She followed his gaze. There, trailing over a branch of a cypress tree that had grown amid the pines, was the clean cut end of a rope. 'No.', it balanced on painful breath as realisation struck. Her tears then flowed. She wanted desperately to throw herself on to her beloved's form but, even in the midst of her agony, knew it'd be a mistake. Though, as close relatives all knew she'd be upset, any further display would probably give the game away. She didn't want his name and reputation damaged, especially now when nothing good would be achieved. She'd have to find time to allow her grief full rein when on her own and away from prying eyes. Bernard looked at her, and understanding his meaning, she nodded. It was time to take him back to the house. 'Send for the priest, please, Bernard. I'll be down shortly.' 'Of course, Miss. I am so sorry. I know how close you were.' 'Thank you Bernard. For the time being, I'd like us to keep quiet about how he died. Please tell the others.' 'I will Miss.'

She watched as they gently lifted him on to the stretcher they'd quickly made from nearby fallen branches. Her eyes then followed the sad procession as it made its way down the hill. When sure they were out of sight, or rather that she was out of their sight, she turned and headed for the secret cottage. Perhaps? There was no delight now in seeing the little door. She knew he wasn't there. It felt a sacrilege to go in, but she had to make sure. The eerie, claustrophobic silence crowded in on her as she struggled to allow breath in. Shock, disbelief, belief, sorrow, fear, and other painful emotions battled within her. She desperately wanted to stop, to not believe, to wait for the sound of his voice, but she knew there was no time to waste. They'd be expecting her at the house. Shaking off the emotions as best as she could, she immediately headed up the stairs and into the room that had once held so much delight. Now it'd only be memories. Memories she'd have to keep to herself forever. She fought back the tears and the urge to scream as she looked around the room. She'd been right. There, propped against one of the lovely vases, was a folded sheet of paper. Her hands shook as she lifted it down and forced herself to unfold it.

My Darling Ellie, My Life breath, My Reason for living. There is no life for me without you, and there can be no life for either of us without our beloved Lord. It has become clear, if we continue, He will have to abandon us. I cannot do that to you. You are too precious. I cannot see any alternative. To remain on this earth and to still know you are also on it would be too unbearable.

I am sorry. I know what I am doing is a sin, but to me it is better this way. My only sadness is that we will not be together. My heart is broken and I will forever miss you. There is so much more I would like to say but do not really have the words. I know you will understand. You know me well enough. Better than I know myself.

Please take care of yourself and forgive me.

How do I express the love I have for you? I cannot. But this comes with all the love I have or could ever hope to have.

Your Daniel

P.S. You better destroy this note once you have read it. It would not do for anyone else to get their hands on it.

Unrestrained tears cascaded. Surely they could have found a way. She folded the wet paper and slid it into her dress pocket.

Through her tear blurred vision, she allowed herself one last look round the room that she would never be able to see again.

13

SUSPICION

'Oh, sorry Miss, I thought you'd gone to the top field. I just popped in to give your room a quick dust.' 'That's alright Doris. I was just taking a few moments before going. You carry on.' 'Thank you Miss, if you're sure?' 'Yes, it's fine Doris, don't mind me.' Grateful she'd just returned Daniel's note to her little box of treasures. She'd not the heart to destroy it, though she'd read it so often she knew it by heart. But it was the last thing he'd touched and given to her. She stood to give herself a last check in the mirror. 'Oh, sorry Miss.' Looking round, she saw Doris had knocked her little box to the floor. On top of the spread contents was Daniel's note. Thankfully, it was face down, so there was no chance of Doris recognising the handwriting. She rushed across and picked up the strewn mementoes before the abashed Doris could. 'Don't worry Doris. I shouldn't have left it hanging over the edge of the dressing table.' 'Sorry Miss, it was an accident.' 'I know, Dorris, please don't upset yourself. These things happen. You can leave the rest of the room. It's not that dusty anyway. You do such a good job of keeping it clean.' Doris's sheepish expression changed to one of delight in a matter of seconds. 'Thank you, Miss.' 'You better see how they're getting on with lunch or we'll have a group of angry workmen howling for their food.' 'Ha, ha, yes Miss. Thank you.' Almost curtseying as she left the room. He'd been right. It was foolish and dangerous to keep his note. Tears rose as she considered its destruction. At least she'd memorised it. She'd never forget his words, no matter how long she lived. If only they could be together again. Perhaps The Lord would forgive and allow them to at least see each other one more time.

Increasingly, it became clear many suspected there'd been more to their relationship than merely being cousins. Gossip, as it will in a small community, abounded, but no one dare speak the thought openly. Ellie's respected family name and considerable wealth made anyone who even thought of the idea hesitate. There was no proof and it could backfire. Rural people could be unforgiving.

'Sorry to interrupt, Miss, but Mrs Combs has just called. I've shown her into the morning room.' 'Thank you Dorris, I'll be straight down.' 'Very well, Miss. I'll let her know.'

'Good morning Mrs Combs, what a delight to have you call.' 'I have only just heard the awful news. About your cousin, I mean.' Her hopes of keeping what had happened quiet for a while longer now evaporated. She should've known it'd not stay a secret for long. 'I came to offer my personal condolences. I know how close you had become.' Her slightly raised eyebrow indicating clearly her thought of them having been "too" close. 'Thank you, that's very kind of you. Yes, we had become close', deciding to take the challenge face on, 'he was really my only remaining close relative. I know I have my uncle and aunt, but they hardly ever visit. It was good to have someone close by.' 'Yes, you mentioned that before. What are you going to do now?' 'What do you mean?' 'Well my dear, while he was about at least you had a man to look out for you. Who will protect you from all those fortune hunters now? It is well known that you are a very wealthy woman. Unscrupulous men will no doubt start turning up on your doorstep, if you get my meaning.' 'Quite clearly Mrs Combs.', trying to control her irritation with little success, 'I think I am now old enough, and hopefully wise enough, to handle them.' 'What about the estate? I imagine your cousin helped you run it and the business.' 'Actually, he didn't. I have taken care of both myself.' 'I see, but really dear you should have a man take over now.' 'Why?' 'It is the way of things, dear. It is the normal path the life of a lady like yourself should follow.' 'I don't see why. Why can't I manage them for myself? Why does everyone think it has to be a man? Daddy taught me much and left me to deal with many of the contracts and issues on my own. He was happy with what I did. In fact, the business has progressed and become even more successful.' 'A young woman like you should be thinking of marriage and a family, not about business and estates.' 'Again, I ask why? Why does everyone presume marriage is the only course for a woman? Why can't they see that a woman can live a perfectly happy and successful life without a man?' Her frustration now in full evidence. 'I am sorry dear, I did not mean to upset you. Mr George mentioned you had some unusual ideas, and how strongly you felt about them.' 'I didn't mean to be rude, Mrs Combs, but I do get annoyed with the narrow-minded views of so many in our society. We no longer live in the dark ages. A woman is no longer a piece of chattel. We are not meant to be a man's possession. We are individuals in our own right. We should be permitted to live the way we choose and not by the dictates of men, convention, or social protocol.' 'Goodness, you really do feel strongly about this.' 'Yes, I do.' 'Are you therefore planning on remaining a spinster?' 'I see nothing wrong with it if I do, but none of us knows what the future holds.' She threw the last bit in as an appeasement and hopefully to bring this unpleasant thread of conversation to a close. She had, in fact, made up her mind she'd never marry. As she'd been the only one for Daniel, he'd been the only one for her. If that could not happen, which of course it couldn't now, then that was it. 'I admire your strength of feeling and character, but if you do remain a spinster, you know it will be difficult. People will not understand. They will think there is something seriously wrong with you. They may even think you have offended our Lord and are being punished.' 'Yes, I do understand. It's a shame people, especially women, are so shortsighted, but whatever happens in my life with respect to marriage or not will be at my choosing, no one else's.' 'I hope you have not minded me raising the point. I had no intention of causing offence or upsetting you. It is just that I am concerned for you, and now you have neither parent thought it wise to raise the matter. Anyway, the whole point of my calling was to offer my condolences. I am truly sorry for your loss.' 'Thank you Mrs Combs, for both your condolences and concerns. As I hope you're now able to see, I'm quite at terms with the latter. The first will take a while.' 'I have no wish to interfere but please remember, if you ever need or wish to talk about anything, I am always here.' 'Thank you, you're very kind.' With that, Mrs Combs bestowed a friendly smile and left.

14

PUNISHMENT?

'He was such a nice man.' 'I've never known such a thoughtful, caring doctor.' 'He truly made all our lives richer.' 'He'll be greatly missed.' 'Such a sad end.' 'My deepest sympathy.' 'Condolences my dear.' Most of the village attended the funeral. He'd become such a recognised part of their society. Ellie, alongside her uncle, aunt, and remaining cousin, thanked people for their considerations.

Deciding what to tell Daniel's parents had troubled her for days. She couldn't tell them the truth. They'd be shocked, and she didn't wish to tarnish the love and respect they had for their son. 'I don't know. He often felt he wasn't doing enough for his patients and the village in general. Maybe that had a part to play.' 'Was there no note?' 'Not as far as I'm aware.' 'Strange, you'd think he'd at least want us to understand.' 'I'm sorry. I don't know what to say.' 'Surly he must have given you some idea. You seemed so close.' 'We were. He's, he'd, been a true support since Daddy's passing.' 'He didn't give you any clue? Was there no sign of something wrong?' 'There must've been, but I evidently missed it.' Not an entire untruth. Though they'd had the conversation about his concern for what their Lord appeared to want, it'd never crossed her mind he do anything drastic. Not at least without talking to her first. But then would he've told her he was going to take his own life?

When his parents and brother returned to the city, Ellie was finally able to sit and contemplate her future. Inwardly she wished she'd no future and The Lord would take her without delay. Should she follow suit? In her heart and soul, she wanted to, but everything in her screamed not to. If there was any chance of them being permitted to see each other again, a second suicide would undoubtedly negate the possibility. It wasn't worth the risk. She'd have to go on without him. She'd have to live whatever life God ordained. Her one consolation, to have Daniel's love in her heart. It'd remain there forever. Nothing would or could diminish that. No matter how wrong anyone considered it. It was still genuine and would always be. 'I hope you won't be cross with me Lord, or you Mummy and Daddy. I can't help what I feel. I still love him, as I do you all.'

Though there'd been more than a few offers, and some unpleasant attempts to persuade her otherwise, marriage to anyone other than Daniel could not be contemplated. Ellie remained a spinster. Mrs Combs had been more than right. It was difficult. Not having Daniel beside her was bad enough, but the small-minded attitudes, especially of the women, made it doubly worse. She'd expected at least some of them to appreciate one of their own proving to men, and society, a woman could be independent. That a woman had value in her own right and didn't need a man to define her. That they were acceptable as individuals for who they were. It proved a forlorn hope. Some were openly hostile, while others would simply quietly cross the street to avoid her. It was clear there were those who'd love to drive her from the village, but her name and wealth and the fact many traded with her prevented any attempt to fulfil such a desire.

It was a primarily lonely life, though she had the companionship of her staff and estate workers, all of whom she still considered extended family members. She'd given them the option to leave if they wished, with full pay and letters of recommendation. Whether any guessed at what had been going on with Daniel, she had no idea, but each one had clearly stated their intent to remain with her.

At times, to keep going became a struggle. What was it all for? She'd never have children and there wasn't anyone to really keep the business going for. It would all naturally pass to Daniel's parents or brother, though she knew full well they weren't that interested. He'd been right about his brother preferring city life and of how good a company manager he'd be. They'd now effectively left Bernard, and eventually his replacement, with their estates only asking a small percentage of the financial proceeds to be sent to them once a year. That was all on trust. They never came to check.

The years passed, and Ellie slowly aged. She did sometimes ask, 'Why dear Lord have you left me on this earth for so long?' When declining health entered, she'd further ask, 'Is this a punishment for our love? Are You extending my life on purpose?' There was never an answer. It became a sorrowful life as she had to watch each of her friends pass away until she was finally left alone, unable to walk and virtually blind. She finally had to seek someone to care for her, but hardly any were willing. In the end she had no option, other than starve, to concede to a couple's unwarranted demand that to take care of her they first wanted all her estate and wealth handed over to them. They were a harsh, greedy, uncaring couple. Ellie was naturally reluctant, but could find no one else willing to help her.

Year after year, they left her bedridden in her darkened, now dilapidated home. Ellie had always been hygienic but now she was left unwashed, with tangled hair and not even a pair of scissors to cut her painful toenails with. All the family possessions had been quality, but had disappeared piece by piece. Their only attempt at so-called care was a once a day visit, with a small plate of unpleasant, unhealthy food. They never even brought any of the fruit Ellie loved, despite the estate being laden with so much.

Ellie died alone in darkness and sorrow. Was this sorrowful, extended life a punishment? Did she ever see her love again?

AFTERWORD

This story is based on real events. Though imagination has had to be employed to envision some scenarios, it, in essence, is an authentic account of what these two lovers had to endure. The account of Ellie's *(not her real name)* last years is also true. It is sad to see how mean and uncharitable people can be.

How many of us have ever been privileged to know such a deep, genuine, all-encompassing love? Too few, I think. Is it as Alfred Lord Tennyson put it in his poem 'In Memoriam', "*Tis better to have loved and lost than never to have loved at all.*". I leave that for you to decide.

Tragedy is a frequent component of life. Though it often results in the end for some, it does not mean the end of life for all those involved, though it can mark the rest of their days, and usually does.

— · —

ABOUT THE AUTHOR

Sophia Venboue is a quiet observer of life who has undertaken a variety of low-key employments to support herself through the years. The wonder of nature is a huge delight to her. Gardening is her favourite occupation when not at work. She considers the marvel of how a tiny seed can grow into the most amazing of plants, nothing short of miraculous. And that she has had a part in it thrills her. Quietly sitting and writing is her other enjoyment.

www.ingramcontent.com/pod-product-compliance
Lightning Source LLC
Chambersburg PA
CBHW020316130626
46549CB00003B/899